OF KISSES AND WISHES

LANA PECHERCZYK

Copyright © 2023 Lana Pecherczyk
All rights reserved.

Of Kisses and Wishes was first published in the Warlords, Witches and Wolves Anthology.

Ebook ISBN: 978-1-922989-19-2
Print ISBN: 9798758006665

This is a work of fiction. Names, characters, businesses, places, events and incidents are either the products of the author's imagination or used in a fictitious manner. Any resemblance to actual persons, living or dead, or actual events is purely coincidental.

Text copyright © Lana Pecherczyk 2021
Cover design © Lana Pecherczyk 2023

www.lanapecherczyk.com

BLURB

Wolfish Anise has always been teased for being a lesser fae of Elphyne. She wishes for two things: the kisses of a long-time friend who never dates outside his breed and to find the elusive Ice-Witch, who promises to give Anise magic and the ability to shift.

Caraway left his pacifist family to join the Guardians and became a ruthless protector of Elphyne. He wants to prove his oxen-shifter breed can be more than docile prey, but two years ago, he failed at protecting the most important fae in his life—his best friend Anise.

When a new mission forces them together on a quest, secret desires are revealed—but have they been revealed too late? Even if Caraway can stop Anise from making the worst mistake of her life, no one walks away from the Ice-Witch with their soul intact.

THE ORDER OF THE WELL

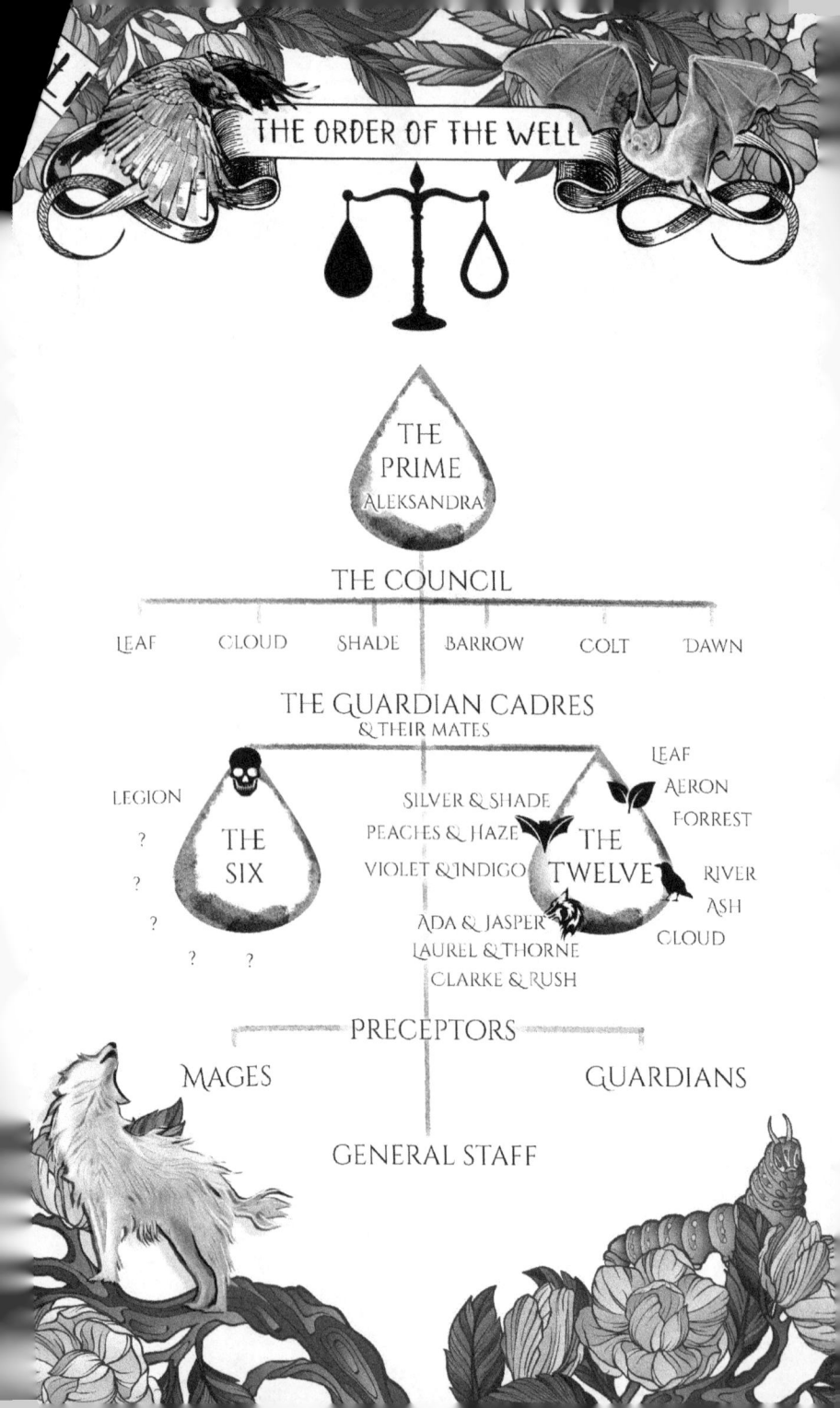

THE PRIME
ALEKSANDRA

THE COUNCIL

LEAF   CLOUD   SHADE   BARROW   COLT   DAWN

THE GUARDIAN CADRES
& THEIR MATES

THE SIX
LEGION
?
?
?
? ?

THE TWELVE
SILVER & SHADE
PEACHES & HAZE
VIOLET & INDIGO
ADA & JASPER
LAUREL & THORNE
CLARKE & RUSH

LEAF
AERON
FORREST
RIVER
ASH
CLOUD

PRECEPTORS

MAGES   GUARDIANS

GENERAL STAFF

WINTER COURT
ACONITE CITY

ICE WITCH

ACONITE SEA

THE ICE FOREST

HUMAN TERRITORY

UNSEELIE KINGDOM
SEELIE KINGDOM

CRYSTAL CITY

RUSH'S CABIN

MEANDER WOODS

WHISPERING WOODS

CRESCENT HOLLOW

- OBSIDIAN MINE
- OBSCENDIA
- CLAW BASIN
- THE ORDER OUTPOST
- AUTUMN COURT
- RUBRUM CITY
- CORNUCOPIA TRADE CITY
- FENRYSFIELD
- THE CEREMONIAL LAKE
- THE ORDER OF THE WELL
- DELPHINIUM CITY
- SPRING COURT
- HELIANTHUS CITY
- SUMMER COURT

Before You Read...

This novella story occurs between books 2 and 3 of the Season of the Wolf Trilogy but can be read as a stand-alone.

There are very mild spoilers in the back (y'all know this is a romance series, so it won't be surprising to see that the couples from books 1 and 2 have had a happy ever after.)

This story was first published in the *Warlords, Witches and Wolves Anthology.*

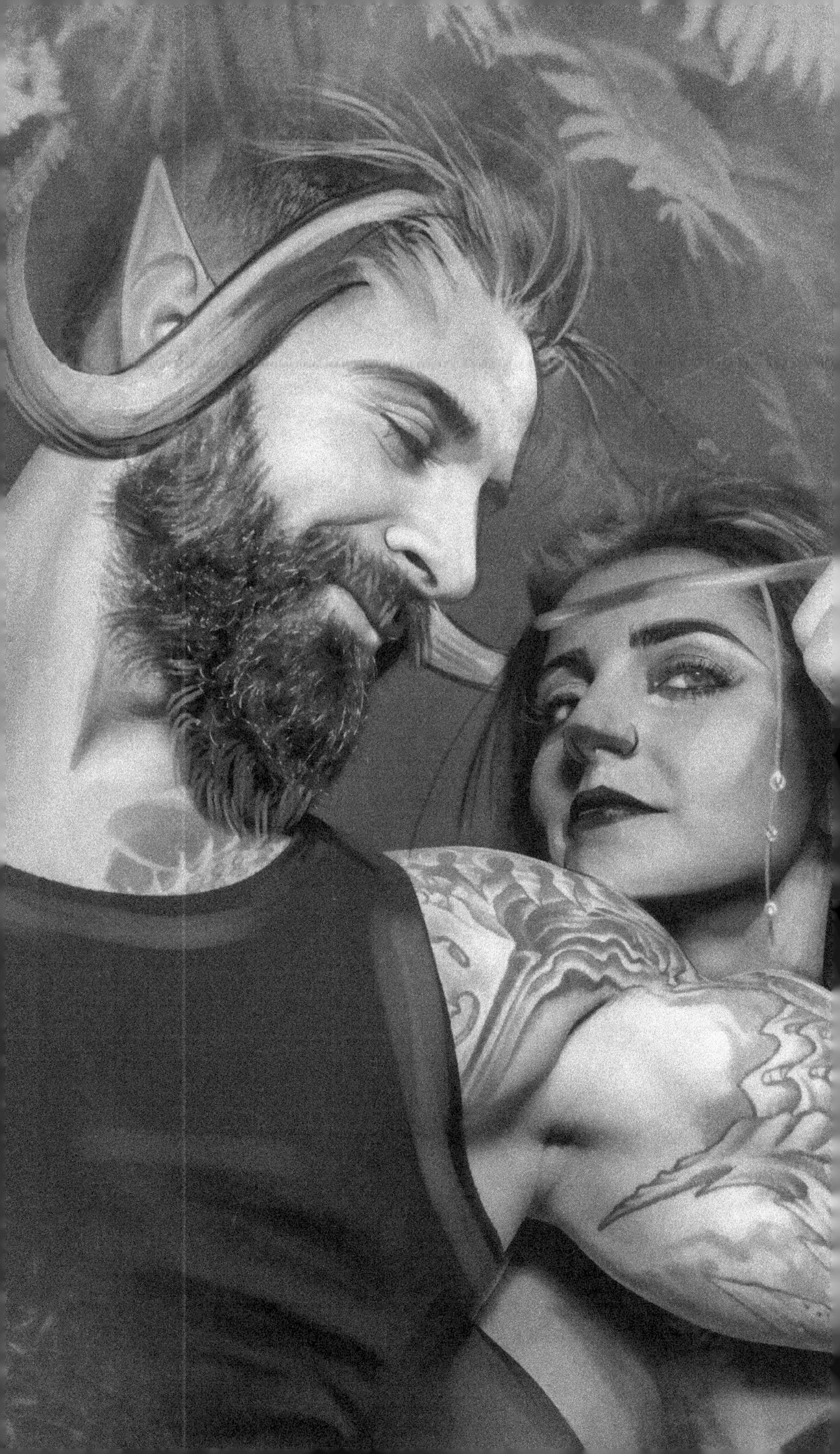

CHAPTER 1

Glass coin tinkled as it landed in Anise's hand. She counted, and then checked down the length of the bar to see if her coworkers watched. Once sure she was free, she pocketed the amount instead of adding it to the Birdcage's nightly takings. She reached beneath the bar and pulled out a small vial of red glowing liquid. Forcing a smile on her face, she handed it to the awaiting female wolf-shifter with wide, earnest eyes.

"You get caught with this outside of Cornucopia, you didn't get it from me. Understood?" Anise warned.

The female smiled tightly, looked down at the tail swishing behind Anise, and struggled to hide her disgust. "I know the deal."

Anise scowled back, immediately on the defense. Any fae who stared at her tail like it was monstrous, classed themselves superior to those *lesser fae*, those like Anise

who appeared different to humans, but held no mana from the Well, and thus couldn't shift or use magic. Lesser fae were considered only one step away from animals.

The shouts of cruel children surfaced from Anise's memories.

"Without your tail and ears, you're basically human!"

"Take that back!"

"You can't shift. You can't hunt. You can't even protect your own kind."

"Shut up!"

Sing-song taunts. "Human. Dirty, dirty human!"

"If you don't stop, I'll tell on you."

"Who will save you? You have no friends."

"Are you going to give me what I paid for, or what?"

Anise's gaze returned to the white-haired female shifter. Like all wolf-shifters, her fur-tipped pointed ears gave her away. She also had an unremarkable body squeezed into a straight dress that hugged her skinny frame. And she smelled like wolf beneath all that perfume. There was nothing special about her, yet she clearly thought so. Probably the daughter or a distant cousin of some high fae Summer Court lord.

"What are you dumb as well as less?" The female snatched the vial from Anise's hand, unstoppered the cork, and downed the contents in one hit.

"Easy there." Anise flinched. "You didn't even wait for the right dose."

"I didn't come to Cornucopia for the right dose. Just like you didn't come here to feel like the second-rate

citizen you are. I've taken Scarlixir before. I have plenty of elves as friends. I know exactly what I'm doing."

Anise had to bite her lip to avoid scoffing. Elves may have been the original fae who'd concocted the elixir, but they had no idea how the magical and inebriating *mana*-infused mixture had been cut and diluted with other chemicals to save coin in production. Anise didn't even know. She had to go by what the dealer had told her. They didn't call it Scarlixir for the scarlet color. No. It was because if you overdosed on the euphoric inducing drug, it made you want to claw your skin until it bled. Hence, the scars.

"Suit yourself." Anise smirked and watched the wolf sashay away to the dance floor. "Ooh, you're going to be paying for that later, too."

She glanced up. The three-story verdant nightclub overflowed with greenery. The central column reached all the way to the ceiling where a hole revealed the night sky. The crescent moon had crossed to the other side of the observatory. If she'd looked five minutes later, she'd have missed it, and the signal that her shift was over.

Elation lifted her soul. Finally. She'd been waiting for this moment for five years. Time to go on vacation. She patted the coin in her pocket. There was enough for where she needed to go, but that last sale was the icing on the cake.

Bidding adieu to her co-workers, Anise collected her jacket from the staffroom and checked her bone dagger was safely strapped to her belt before heading home. Not

only was the dagger reinforced with mana to make it stronger, but she'd paid extra to spell it to always hit its mark. It cost a fortune, but after she was attacked two years ago and held hostage, she liked to feel secure.

The walk home to her modest apartment was not a safe one, but there were no safe parts of town. Cornucopia was not ruled by any fae kingdom, neither Seelie nor Unseelie. It existed as a neutral territory where all fae-kind could come together. No rules applied. Well, not many. Those rules were enforced by the Order of the Well, who were more like the magic police in terms of offenses to the integrity of the Well. If you were like Anise and held no mana with which to pervert, or held no forbidden metals or plastics, you weren't even a fly in their swamp. The only other law was that of The Ring, a gladiator-style pit where you solved your differences.

Lucky for Anise, she'd kept to herself during her stay. She'd only left her home town of Crescent Hollow because it was no longer safe there either. As the closest fae settlement to the humans in the wasteland, she'd met the unfortunate fate of being kidnapped and tortured two years earlier. The ringleader of this torture was the Alpha of Crescent Hollow at the time, Lord Thaddeus Nightstalk. He'd been secretly working with humans to bargain for metal cages and weapons so he could control Guardians—the mana-enhanced warriors who worked for the Order of the Well. As part of the deal, Thaddeus had also tortured many of the lesser fae residents of Crescent Hollow, Anise included.

It was pure cowardice. Not only had Thaddeus picked those fae who were more vulnerable, but he also sucked dry what little mana they had so he could give it to the humans for their own nefarious purposes. It was Anise's only blessing to have no mana to give.

Shivering with reasons nothing to do with the cold, Anise kept her hand poised over her dagger and her eyes wary. Every shadow and insect scuttle made her jolt. By the time she made it to her place, she was a bag of raw nerves. Once inside the one-room apartment, she double bolted the door and lit a candle. Not only did she check every dark crevice of the room, but also beneath the bed. Once satisfied, she crossed to the window, tweaked the drapes, and peeped outside into the dark alley street. Her room was on the second floor, and there was no other way to get into the room other than the front door.

After she washed her face, she pulled the pillows from her bed and stuffed them under the covers so it looked like someone slept there. Then she unsheathed her dagger, got to her knees, and crawled beneath the bed. There she had set up her own little den. A woolen blanket, another pillow, and a collection of her most precious items. A box with her saved coins, a dried flower her friend Caraway had once given her, and a secret invitation addressed to Anise from the Ice-Witch. Her salvation.

Clutching her dagger, she settled and tried not to let the darkness bring the wails and screams from her night-

mares. The memories of being trapped in a cage, elevated from the ground, starved, and emaciated.

Two weeks.

She'd been held hostage for two weeks. Little food. Little water. And no one came to save her. Not even the one friend she thought she had.

"Who will save you? You have no friends."

Anise sniffed and wiped her nose with the back of her hand. Cradling it to her chest, she clutched the Ice-Witch's invitation until she fell asleep.

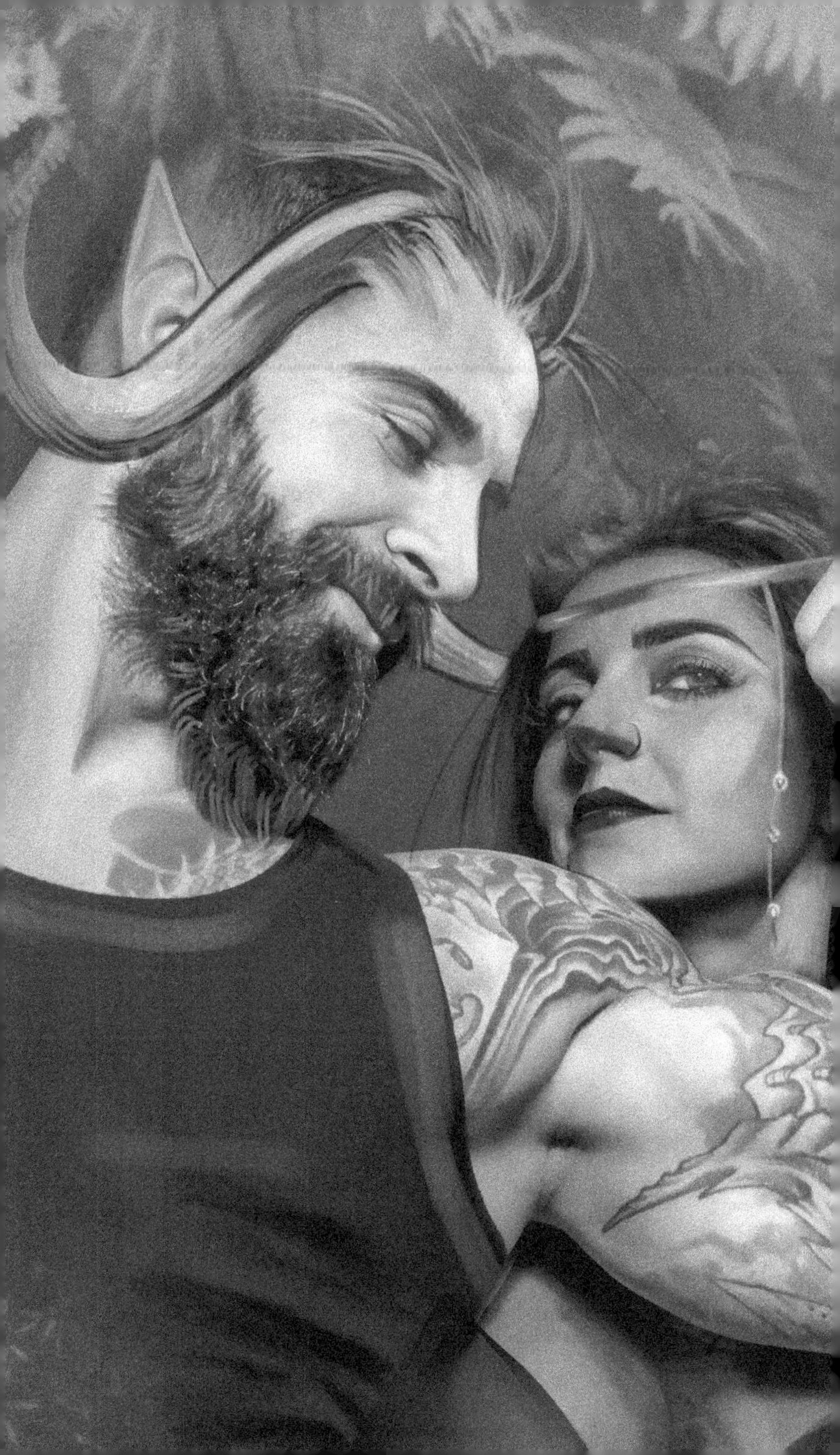

CHAPTER 2

*C*araway always fancied himself a big fae. As a muskox shifter, he towered above most others at an inch over seven-feet tall. Taller than even the legendary Guardians in the Cadre of Twelve. Caraway's big bones and large frame were stacked with slabs of hard muscle honed from decades of heavy training under the tutelage of the Order's ruthless preceptors.

All manner of fae shrunk when he arrived in his black leather Guardian uniform. And most looked in fear at his sharp, curved horns as they flowed from the top of his head, then down and out at his cheeks. But it was truly the giant metal broadsword strapped to his back that incited the most knee-knocking terror. One cleave of his mighty blade, Reckoning, and any creature in Elphyne would be cut in half. Metal had the ability to not only halt magic in its tracks but pierce almost any manner of

surface. Apart from the Guardians, who'd earned their endorsement through a painstaking ceremony, no other fae was sanctioned to carry metal. Touching the forbidden substance would cut their magic supply from the Well and cause a painful headache.

But not Caraway. Not the Guardians. They could decimate the enemy *and* use the full force of the gifts the Well had given them. This dual power made them nigh unstoppable in Elphyne.

So he should feel tall. He should feel big. Invincible. But standing where he was, on the Guardian training field at the Order, with the sun blinding him, and facing one of the Twelve, he felt like a four-foot-tall dwarf.

Facing him from about ten feet away was Rush, a wolf-shifter who'd recently mated with Clarke, a human who inexplicably had, and could use, mana. She'd been exposed to the Well over a two-thousand-year sleep, frozen in ice. She thawed a few years ago and brought with her news of an evil human who'd caused the destruction of the old world and had awoken in this time with the intent to reclaim Elphyne's resources for himself.

Clarke was Rush's, Well-blessed mate.

That meant the silver-haired shifter in front of Caraway, was not only lethal because he could rip Caraway to shreds with sharp teeth, or slice Caraway with his sword, but also blast him with endless offensive magic without running out of power. If his stores of mana were low, all he needed to do was siphon some from his powerful mate. Rush was indestructible.

How was Caraway going to fight that?

"You're a disgrace to the herd," Caraway's mother's voice filtered from his memories. "Us muskox don't fight. We don't spill blood. We live in harmony with the Well."

And when a human raiding party had invaded his family's territory, their pacifist ways could do nothing to protect their kind. Half their herd had been wiped out. But did losing so many lives make Caraway's mother change her mind? No. She still looked on in disgust as he left on his way to submit to the Guardian initiation.

"Are you going to stand there all day staring into space, or spar with me?" Rush laughed, scratching his gray beard.

The Guardian hadn't yet released his sword. The handle poked over his shoulder, taunting Caraway.

Caraway's grip tightened on his own sword, Reckoning. He narrowed his eyes and then charged. Heavy feet thudded across the grass.

Rush pushed his palm out, the blue Well-blessed markings on his hand glowed brightly, and a gust of sharp, cold wind came at Caraway. Like a wall, the element hit and knocked him backward. He landed hard on his rear, jarring the senses out of him.

"Use your sword," Rush shouted back. "It's broad enough the metal will displace the mana I send your way."

Gritting his teeth, Caraway planted Reckoning's tip into the grass and used it to lever himself up. Well-damn it. This was embarrassing. Get him in hand-to-hand

combat and he would come out on top. But he needed this. The extra training.

The human enemies emerging didn't play by the rules, and he needed to be ready. He'd failed too many times already.

Anise's smirking face came to mind and he almost lost his footing. Cute wolfish ears twitching in irritation, dark stain on her nose, big golden eyes with long sweeping lashes. Something squeezed hard in his chest. His old friend had moved away and hadn't told him where, which meant she didn't want to be found. He couldn't blame her. He'd fucked up.

"Stop!" A male shout came from the sidelines.

Caraway squinted into the sun, shielded his eyes. The team leader of the Twelve, Leaf, a golden-haired elf with a superiority complex, waved him over. Leaf was also a council member. This could mean only one thing.

Caraway had a mission.

Wiping the dirt off Reckoning, Caraway sheathed the great sword at the baldric on his back and then strode over. Leaf, Rush, and his son Thorne almost converged to meet. Fae stopped aging at about the age of twenty years, so both father and son looked almost identical except for their eyes and hair. Rush's eyes were golden, and Thorne's were icy blue. Rush's hair was long and silver, Thorne's was buzzed at the sides and short on top. All three looked at Caraway ominously.

Why were they looking at him like that? As though he wasn't about to like what they said next.

"What is it?" he asked.

Leaf folded his arms, his black leathers creaking. "Cloud has finished interrogating the human who worked with High King Mithras."

"Oh?" Caraway raised his brow and did his best to hide his blatant disgust for both the Seelie High King and the human he'd conspired with. The same human who'd manipulated and worked with the fae who'd tortured Anise for two weeks. "Does that mean we can kill him now?"

Thorne shot Caraway dark eyes. A feral glint shone back at Caraway, and the pacifist in his blood wanted to shrink back. Oxen and Wolves were enemies in the animal world, but Caraway had found this one to be his greatest ally.

Thorne bared his fangs. "The prisoner is mine."

Caraway folded his arms. "That human tortured Anise."

"He tortured my mate first. If there's anything left of him after I've had him, he's all yours."

Caraway bit back a retort, because Thorne was well within his rights to take revenge on the human. Laurel was Thorne's Well-blessed mate. They shared not only mana but emotions. Thorne would have relived Laurel's pain as though it were his own. Anise wasn't Caraway's mate. She might not even be his friend.

Not after she blamed him for failing to notice she'd been locked in a cage for two weeks. That tightness in his chest constricted again.

"I hate to burst your bubbles," Leaf drawled. "But neither of you will get your hands on him yet. Cloud has failed to draw worthy information from the human. His mind is locked tight like a vise. Cloud is finished with his interrogation, but we have other methods we will try next. There is one lead we need you to investigate, Caraway."

Caraway looked at the other three, more capable Guardians. All of them were part of the Twelve, the most feared and revered warriors of the Order of the Well. Each of them vicious and uniquely powerful in their own way, it was every Guardian's dream to one day earn their place in the tight-knit cadre of brothers-in-arms. Not only were they powerful, but two of them had already attained a status all Guardians secretly wanted but denied they did—they had found love in this impossible world.

Up until now, it was assumed the life of a Guardian was lonely and empty when it came to mating. Long term relationships weren't encouraged. Not only was a Guardian's duty demanding, but dangerous. Lives were often cut short. Short dalliances were encouraged.

Until recently.

Thorne had worked on abolishing the unsanctioned breeding law. Rush had a two-year-old daughter that ran around the Order campus. Times were certainly changing.

"Why me?" Caraway asked. "Clearly I'm not the most experienced in this group."

"But you have the best connection to the person who has the information."

"Who?"

"Anise."

Caraway's heart stuttered. His mouth dried. *They'd found her?* "You want me to interrogate her?"

"No," Leaf replied. "None of that. But we want you to infiltrate her journey. Go where she is going and conduct your own investigation."

"I'm not following."

"She's been invited to see the Ice-Witch."

As though the hag was standing next to him, Caraway's bones froze. The Ice-Witch was a powerful sorceress who, not only made the most heinous magical bargains with fae, but did so without scruples or discrimination. Every Guardian knew you didn't bargain with the witch unless you were prepared to offer your soul and submit to eons of torture. If you came out of her ice cave with anything less, then you were having a good day.

But did Anise know this?

"The witch is a powerful adversary," Caraway said. "Any of the cadre would do a better job."

"It's Anise," Thorne replied with a soulful gaze. "It was me who pulled her from that cage, Caraway. But it was you she called for. If she's heading to the Ice-Witch, then... she's going to need a friend."

Caraway swallowed the lump in his throat and he stared hard at the ground, trying not to let the burn behind his eyelids overflow into tears. Anise had asked for

him, even after he'd failed to realize she was in trouble. He'd left Crescent Hollow before she'd been taken because Anise and he had argued. She was fed up with the red-coated royal Seelie guards causing havoc every time they came to town. She was fed up with the town's Lord and Alpha, Thaddeus, ruling the village so cruelly. And she was frustrated that no one took her seriously as a lesser fae. As usual, Caraway had stayed out of the unrest. Guardians were forbidden to get involved with general fae politics. If it didn't involve mana, then it wasn't their problem.

Guardians were a dying breed and the war against warped magic and keeping the integrity of the Well alive was growing every day. They simply didn't have enough resources to be the police of everything. A line had to be drawn, and fae politics was on the other side.

"How did you find her?" Caraway asked, throat dry.

"You know how Laurel and I got sent to the Ring by causing a disturbance at the Birdcage?" Thorne asked. "We ran into Anise there."

Caraway nodded. The Birdcage was an elixir den in Cornucopia. Fae from all over Elphyne went there to unwind with dance, drink, or to screw, and to satisfy their deviant urges. Being in Cornucopia, the establishment got away without adhering to any laws that restricted revelry in the Seelie or Unseelie Kingdoms. Usually, this freedom leaned toward the hedonistic side, but Caraway had seen darker rooms and cages with strange sadistic goings-on.

That was where Anise had been working?

"We need you to drill the Ice-Witch for information," Leaf continued. "All our prisoner gave us was her name. But it's more than we've received after days of interrogation." Leaf plucked a feather from his shoulder and flicked it to the ground. Then he met Caraway's eyes. "You're authorized to use force if necessary, but if you discover the witch is the source of the perversion of magic the humans have been using, then don't do anything. Bring the information back and we will assess. At the very least, get a location for us."

Granting wishes to make someone taller or more beautiful was one thing, but lately, mana-warped monsters had been emerging all over Elphyne. If the witch was responsible for those, then she would be dealt with by the Order. If she was also the one feeding the humans secrets on how to use mana, then she would rue the day she betrayed her own kind.

Something else occurred to Caraway. "What would Anise want with the Ice Witch?"

"What does anyone want?" Leaf replied.

Anise's cute tail swished into Caraway's mind and his heart stopped. It was the one thing she'd always been self-conscious about, and he'd bet his sword that she was going to bargain away her soul so she could look like a normal fae.

The two of them had become friends over a mutual bond—they'd both been branded as outcasts. He, for his Guardian status and his family's disdain for violence. She, because she couldn't make the full shift into a wolf. She

couldn't shift at all. It had never bothered Caraway, but he knew she stewed about it.

This was not good. He couldn't let her make this mistake. Anise was perfect, just the way she was born. Becoming a shifter was not worth the damnation of her eternal soul. That was priceless.

"I'll go," Caraway said. "Just tell me where and when."

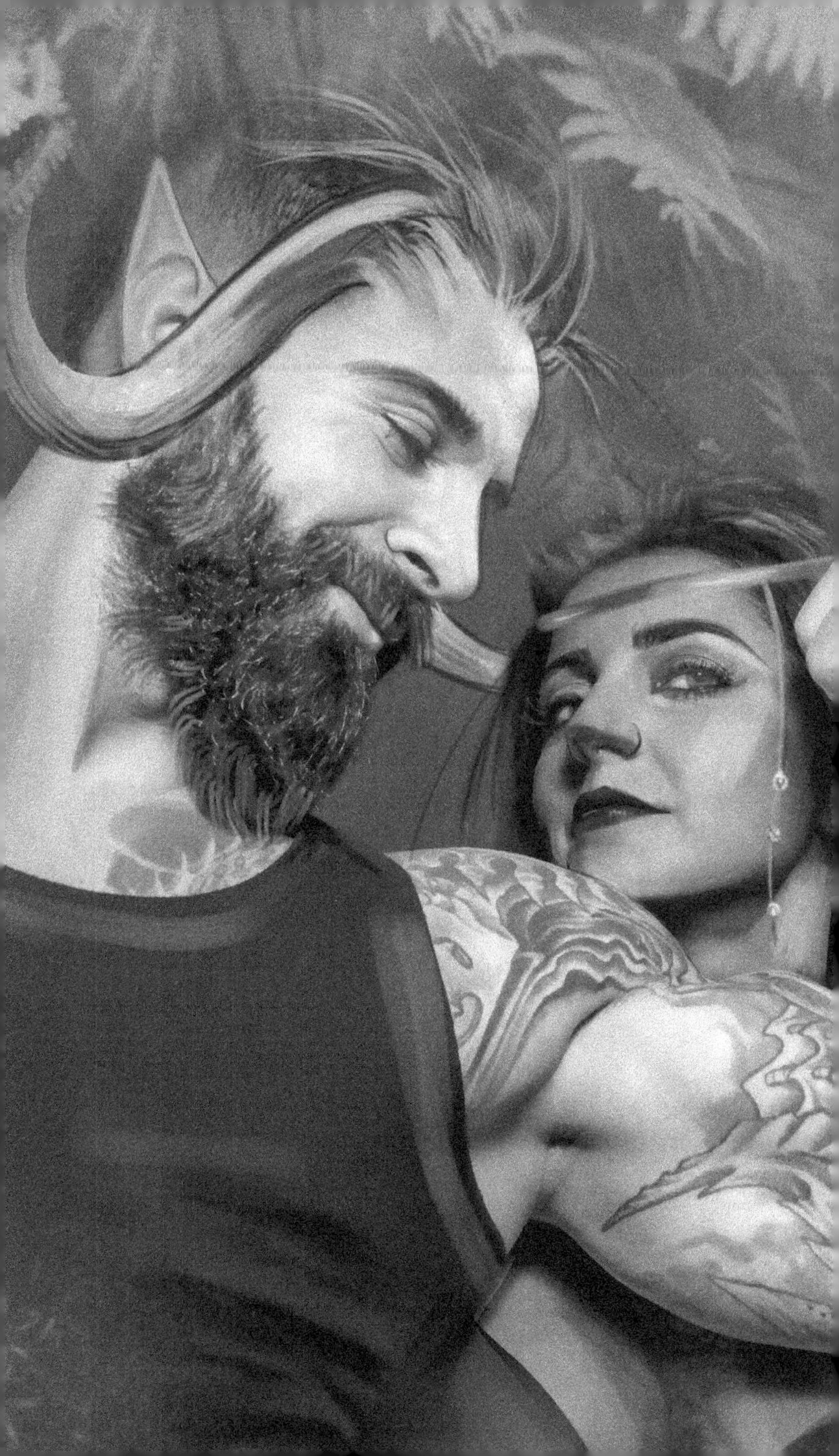

CHAPTER 3

*A*nise woke to the sound of knocking at her door. A peek from beneath the bed showed sun rays had escaped the confines of the curtains to lighten the room. She rubbed her eyes. She should already be awake and on her way by now. Damn it.

Sleeping under the bed felt safer, but it was also darker and she'd missed her dawn wake-up call.

Knock-knock-knock.

Frowning, Anise found her dagger and shimmied out from beneath the bed. Cracking her back, then neck, she eyed the door with suspicion. She'd been living here for over a year but hadn't told anyone. There was no reason she'd have a visitor. She gripped her dagger hard and darted a glance to the window, suddenly cursing the lack of opening for an escape. She supposed she could break the glass.

"Anise?" came the muffled deep voice. "It's me."

Anise stared at the door.

It's me.

Oh, how she'd dreamed of hearing those two little words over and over whilst captured and tortured in that cage. How she'd hoped and longed for them, held onto them as though they were a lifeline.

A lifeline that never came.

The tension in her body shifted until it crumpled her face. She opened the door and scowled despite her heart galloping and her stomach fluttering. *Damn it.*

Caraway loomed in the hallway, his big bulk taking up most of the room. His head and curved horns almost brushed the ceiling. Segmented pauldrons on the Guardian uniform hit the walls on either side—he was that broad. Bone stud buttons ran down the front of his flat torso. Blue piping accentuated the shape of his body—bulging where his biceps stretched the leather jacket almost indecently. A broadsword was holstered over his back.

And the most dangerous part of all—his big, brown, long-lashed doe eyes staring right into her, reaching inside and tugging on her atoms, sending them into a frenzy.

His presence stole Anise's breath away. Nothing had changed in the way her body reacted to him. Only her mind.

She looked closer and took in his face, surprised to note his usual jolly, flushed coloring was gone. Messy shaggy hair fell over his curved horns. Scruff over his

square jaw. Dark, bruised circles beneath those long lashes.

His usual nonchalant vibe had been replaced with hard lines. A pinched look to his face, a flattened press of his lips, and tendons in his temples pulsed from a clenched jaw.

It didn't suit him.

The old Anise wanted to ask what had happened to suck the jolly out of him. The sound of his big-bellied laugh had warmed her on many cold nights during their friendship. But the new Anise, the one he'd left in that cage to rot, didn't give a shit.

"Go away," she said and tried to close the door.

Caraway shoved his giant boot in the gap, stopping it from closing. He put his big meaty hand on the door and pressed. It seemed effortless, and the marked difference in their body strength drove her nuts. This was why she was going to see the Ice-Witch. *This.*

Helplessness swam over her and she stood back. Caraway ducked to get under the doorframe, came in, and closed the door behind him. He surveyed the room with trepidation.

"This is where you've been staying?"

His gaze landed on the pillow decoy in the bed, tilted to see the blanket and sleeping arrangement beneath, and then caught the dagger still in her hand. When his shrewd gaze lifted to meet hers, it softened.

"I don't want your pity, Caraway," she said, pointing the dagger at him, and then the door. "And I told you to

go away. So you should respect a lady's wishes and do just that."

But he didn't go. He started poking around the room as though he owned it. He went to the window, opened the curtain, looked outside, and then tested it to see if it opened. Turning, his eyes tracked around the room until they landed on her knapsack, filled and ready for her journey. His brows lifted.

"Where are you going?"

"None of your business." Anise folded her arms. "Why are you here, Caraway?"

Those brows lowered darkly. "I've been looking for you for a long time, Anise. Why are you running away from me? I thought we were friends."

Her eyes narrowed. "Friends don't leave friends to the mercy of evil, twisted people."

"I didn't know about that until it was too late."

"I told you things were getting dire in that town. I *told* you." The accusation was a spear of vitriol. The moment the words were out of her mouth, Caraway flinched as though hit.

He sat heavily on the bed. It creaked from his weight and the great sword at his back twisted to accommodate the new position. He put his head in his hands.

"I know," he said softly. "But I'm not allowed to get involved with—"

Anise held up her hand. "Oh spare me the same rigmarole. I've heard the Order's mantra before. 'Not mana, not

my problem,' right? You and I both know it goes deeper than that."

She'd meant deeper in the sense that the world wasn't painted in shades of gray, but when Caraway shot her hurt, accusatory eyes, she knew he thought she'd meant something else. She stuttered and sighed. The tension in her body melted. "You know I didn't mean it that way."

"I think you did," he shot back. "You of all people know what my family thinks of me."

She worried her lip with her teeth. A band of guilt wrapped around her chest. When they'd been close friends, Caraway had confessed his darkest shame one night while they were both inebriated. His family was peace-loving. He wanted to save the world and had embraced violence. At least if it was in the name of the Well, he had a higher, holy purpose no one could argue with. If he resorted to helping Anise out and doling out his own version of justice to the humans and other fae reprobates who'd kidnapped her, then the lines were blurred and perhaps he really was this lower-than-low person his family accused him of being. He'd be a monster no different to the mana-twisted beasts he hunted.

The real, open regret on his face plucked at Anise's heart and for the first time, she realized that perhaps those hard lines he'd grown were from her, just another person in his life who'd asked him to make an impossible decision.

She sat down next to him with a heavy sigh and hand-signed an apology. She put a fist to her chest and made a

circle motion. Fae don't voice their thanks or say sorry, for it left them in another's debt. Only family freely spoke these because it was known that true family would do anything for each other, regardless of debt.

Caraway hand-signed his apology too. "I should have been there to protect you, no matter what. You're right. Ignoring the plight of others because it isn't my job isn't a way to live."

"I get it," she soothed. "The Prime doesn't want you to get involved."

He gritted his teeth. "But that's not stopping the Cadre of Twelve. Rush and Thorne have both broken the rules recently. And the Prime's not reprimanded them." He scrubbed his face. "What difference does it make if I'm fighting to preserve the integrity of the Well if the world it goes to is turning to shit?"

Her heart reached out to him. It might have only taken him a few decades, and almost losing her, but he was finally getting it.

"It was also unfair of me to throw the burden of my capture at you," she said. "I know you would have been there if you knew."

He turned to her, eyes brimming with hope. "Can we go back to being friends?"

Her heart lurched. Her hand slid under the cover on the bed and grasped the paper invitation that had consumed her life for the past year and more. Indecision rocked her. What would he think of her choice?

"What's that?" he asked, eyes toward where her hand moved.

Alarmed, she looked down. The white letter poked out from beneath the blanket. There was no way he'd let her go without an explanation, so she took a deep breath, and let it out.

"It's an invitation to see the Ice-Witch."

Silence.

She closed her eyes and waited for the reprimand she knew was coming. Caraway had always been a come as you are kind of male, but while he'd spoken the words, his actions were louder. He'd only dated high fae. She never saw him with a lesser fae. None like her.

Warm, rough fingers touched her cheek. Her eyes flew open and met his. In them, she saw pity. She knocked his hand away and stood up.

"Don't judge me, Caraway."

"I wasn't."

She looked sideways at him. "You weren't?"

"No. But visiting the Ice-Witch for any reason won't have a happy ending. You know this."

Bitter pain and failure swirled in her gut. He had no idea what it was like to be sub-par. To be teased your whole life, first by cruel kids, then by even meaner adults. That last customer at the Birdcage hadn't been a one-off. Fae like her treated Anise differently all the time. It was the tail.

She'd considered cutting it off once, just to be rid of it. But then there was the discoloration on her face. The

darker nose. The black-rimmed eyes. The bigger than normal wolfish ears.

"You know the reason I'm visiting her," she said to him. "And you know the hurt I feel is bone-deep. I'll do anything to be rid of it."

"What are you asking the witch for?" he asked softly.

"I want the ability to shift. To protect myself."

"I'll protect you."

"You can't be there all the time. It's not your job."

He growled, eyes flashing possessively. "It should be. I should never have let you be taken."

"I should be able to protect myself as all the other wolves can."

"There are other ways to keep yourself safe."

"Don't." She held up her hand. "Don't try to dissuade me. I've made up my mind."

A heavy sigh. Then, "If you want to see the Ice-Witch, then I won't stop you."

"You won't?"

"No." He stood, his big body crowding the room. His eyes turned hard. "But I will go with you."

Her lashes flew wide. "But... but you can't. The Prime won't allow it."

"Fuck the Prime," he replied. "I won't leave you unprotected. Not anymore. Do you understand?"

Slowly, she nodded, hardly believing her ears.

"Good. When do we leave?"

She collected her bag and fur-lined cape. "Now."

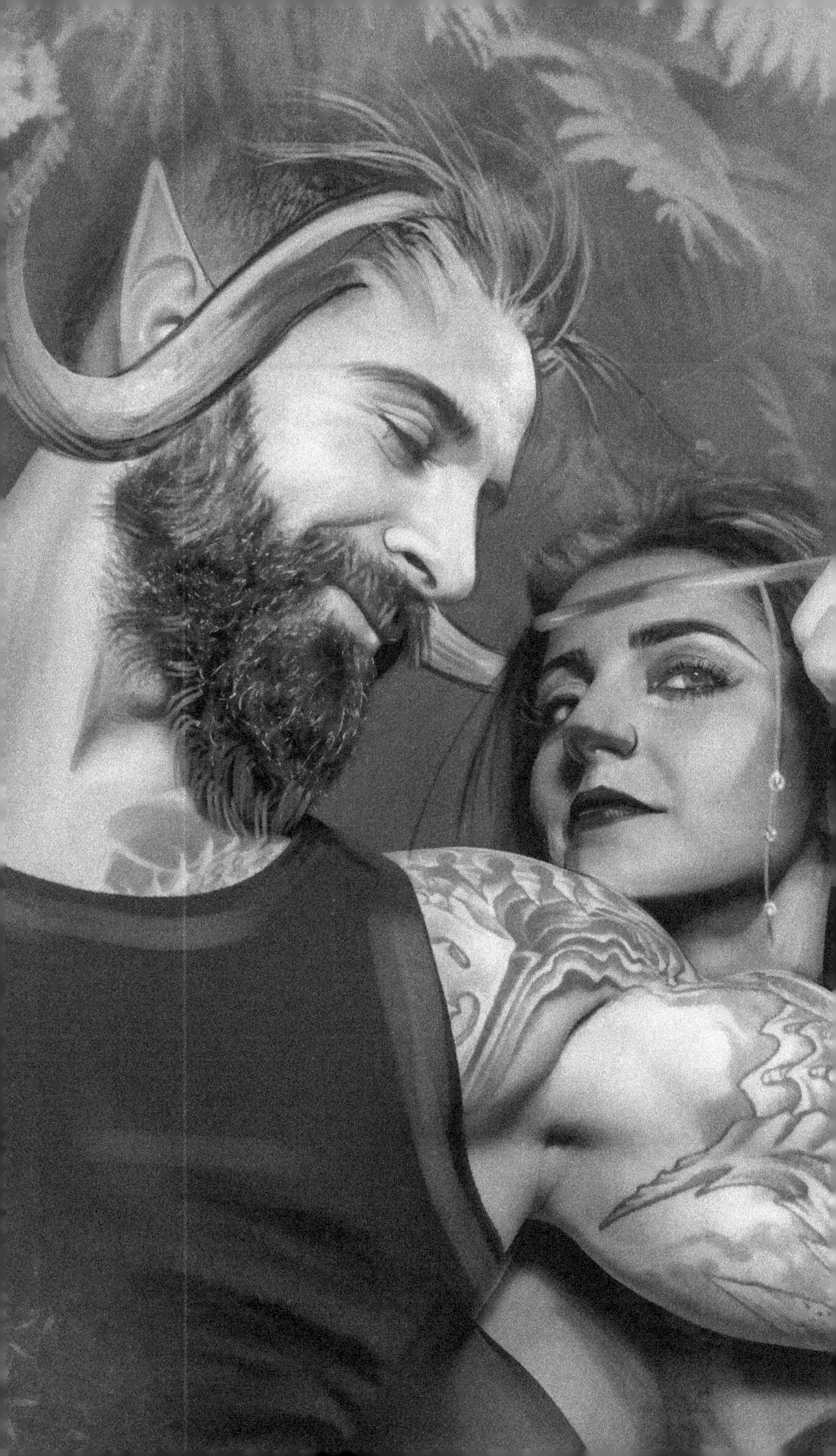

CHAPTER 4

Caraway followed Anise through the Meandering Woods. A smidge of gray sky could be seen through the tall, still wet trees from recent rain. Sticks and twigs crunched and squelched underfoot as they trekked. They'd been walking for two hours, and yet the fallen log marker was nowhere in sight.

The moment Caraway read the letter's instructions, he'd become wary. *Meet a troll at a fallen log, and then be told of the true location of the Ice-Witch?* It seemed preposterous. Trolls were notorious for misdirection. Fae couldn't lie, but they could send you on a wild wolpertinger chase just to mess with your head and then claim it was to reveal your heart's desire. Trolls were also carnivores, and didn't discriminate between their meat. Animal, monster, human, or fae, it was all the same to them. That Anise had planned to go there alone did not sit well with Caraway.

Doubt crept into his mind. He'd been instructed to keep the mission as reconnaissance only, but he would prepare himself for action if necessary.

"How far do we have to go?" Caraway asked.

Anise shot him a sardonic look. "Are you tired, big guy?"

He snorted. "No. I just don't want you to be taken for a fool."

She waved the folded letter. "This prevents that. The gully should be just up ahead."

They cleared bracken and stepped into a ditch, boots landing in soggy leaves. A burst of woodland sprites exploded, fluttering and zipping about, cursing in their high-squeaky voices for him to watch his step. Then, as if hearing something he couldn't, the sprites scattered to the winds.

The hairs on Caraway's arms lifted. He checked around and looked for something... anything. Being so close to Unseelie territory, where the fae of chaos ruled, there were many dangers, not to mention mana-warped monsters.

The ditch he'd stepped into was, in fact, the gully they'd been searching for. It widened ahead and extended into the distance. More lush greenery littered the bottom.

The birds stopped chirping. The insects silenced.

Anise, not picking up the tension in the air, made a jubilant sound and pointed to a moss-covered fallen log.

"That must be it!"

A shadow emerged from behind the log. The troll, a

five-foot gnarly beast, walked on two legs. Its overlong arms extended to the ground where clawed fingers scraped the dirt. His brown fuzzy hair extended from the top of his head and down to his bare back. Pointed ears twitched as his beady eyes watched them approach. Tense posture said he was not to be trifled with, and the scars over his almost naked body proved it. This troll was a survivor.

No weapons, as far as Caraway could see. The troll wore nothing but a torn, dirty loincloth and a necklace made from some sort of leathery dehydrated chunks.

When the troll darted a nervous glance to where Caraway's hand gripped the hilt of his broadsword, Caraway's lip curled but he released and lowered his hand to his side. No good would come of starting this with an altercation. Best to act like there was nothing to be worried about.

Caraway put his boot on a small rock and leaned casually on his knee.

Anise held up her folded letter and raised her voice. "I have an invitation to see the Ice-Witch. It says to come here and you will show me the rest of the way."

The troll squinted at her, then at Caraway. "We don't want no Guardians around here. We eat Guardians."

For a moment, Caraway thought the troll was simply trying to sound threatening, but then he took a closer look at the troll's necklace. Those leather chunks were familiar. *Pointed ears*. Some big, some small, and some child-sized.

Caraway's stomach bottomed out. This troll had eaten children, and it was proud of it. Ice washed through his veins, tensing every muscle.

"Who him?" Anise laughed, pointing at Caraway. "He's not here to cause trouble. He's just my bodyguard for the trip. You won't hear a peep out of him. Right, Car?"

Anise's eyes pleaded with him, and he knew he couldn't jeopardize this mission, not without getting instructions first. He bared his teeth in what he supposed could be called a smile, and then raised his palms to the troll in surrender.

The troll glared at Caraway's glistening blue teardrop tattoo under his right eye—his Guardian mark—then at the sharp horns curling from the top of his head where his gaze lingered. The troll backed away. For a moment, Caraway thought he'd retreated, but then the troll tossed a glance over his shoulder and snarled to Anise, "You coming?"

A grin split her face. Elation brightened her skin. She trotted after the troll, her long dark tail swishing at her rear. It had been a while since Caraway had seen a swish in his friend's tail, and he liked it.

He followed, but unclipped the fastening strap securing Reckoning to his baldric. Now if he needed to draw his magic-cutting weapon, there would be nothing hindering the release.

The troll took them to a cave entrance where bones and body parts hung on strings, curing over a smokey fire. They looked fresh. Two, three, maybe four legs which

equaled *two fae* that had been killed and trussed up. A quick glance around the cave showed no signs of contraband, which made these deaths not Caraway's problem.

Strange items and knick-knacks stacked in high, precarious piles were hoarded around the place, both inside and outside the cave. They were remnants of the old-time before a nuclear winter had swallowed the land and spat out a destitute, icy planet. Glancing deeper into the cave, he caught sight of a straw bed covered with a soft woolen blanket. It looked strange in a rough troll cave.

Something moved in the darkness, and his senses lit up.

Another troll?

He sniffed the air, but his senses weren't as attuned as a wolf's. He glanced at Anise and caught a crease between her brows. She'd smelled something she didn't like, but shook her head and dismissed it.

The troll rifled around in a wicker basket by the cave entrance until he found a portal stone. He grunted at his find and then gestured with urgency for Anise to show him the invitation. Instead of reading it, he sniffed it.

"Yep. Smells like witch," he muttered and then handed Anise the stone. "This will take you to her."

Anise received the stone but slumped. "I can't activate portal stones. Could you do it?"

The troll shook his head. "Not part of the deal. You go now. We hungry."

"I can do it," Caraway offered.

"Good," the troll picked up a long, jagged bone machete that had been resting against the cave. He jabbed it toward Caraway and Anise. "You go."

Caraway frowned at the troll's haste and moved between the sharp bone weapon and Anise.

"Come on," he said. "Let's go do this elsewhere."

He walked Anise out of the gully but, try as he might, he couldn't shake the sensation something was very wrong back at the camp. That blanket. Those curing body parts... He paused just as they climbed out of the gully and into a clearing. Anise handed him the stone, but instead of activating it, he turned back to survey the direction they'd come from.

Smoke curled from the troll's campfire, winding it's way up through the treetops and into the overcast sky.

It had been too easy.

Trolls were evil bastards when they wanted to be. Trying to get one of them to do something for you was a hard task. They were deceptive, too.

And then the cutting sound of a baby's cry pierced through the trees. Caraway's heart leaped into his throat. His eyes locked with Anise's. She'd heard too. But it was the diminishing hope turned resignation in her eyes that broke his heart. And when her ears flattened and she turned her gaze away, he understood that her faith in him was gone.

No words were needed. She'd thought because he was a Guardian, he'd ignore the plight of a baby, just like he'd

failed to pay attention to the signs leading up to her capture two years ago.

He unsheathed Reckoning and growled as he shoved the portal stone at her.

"Stay here and wait for me," he ordered, and then headed back toward the cave.

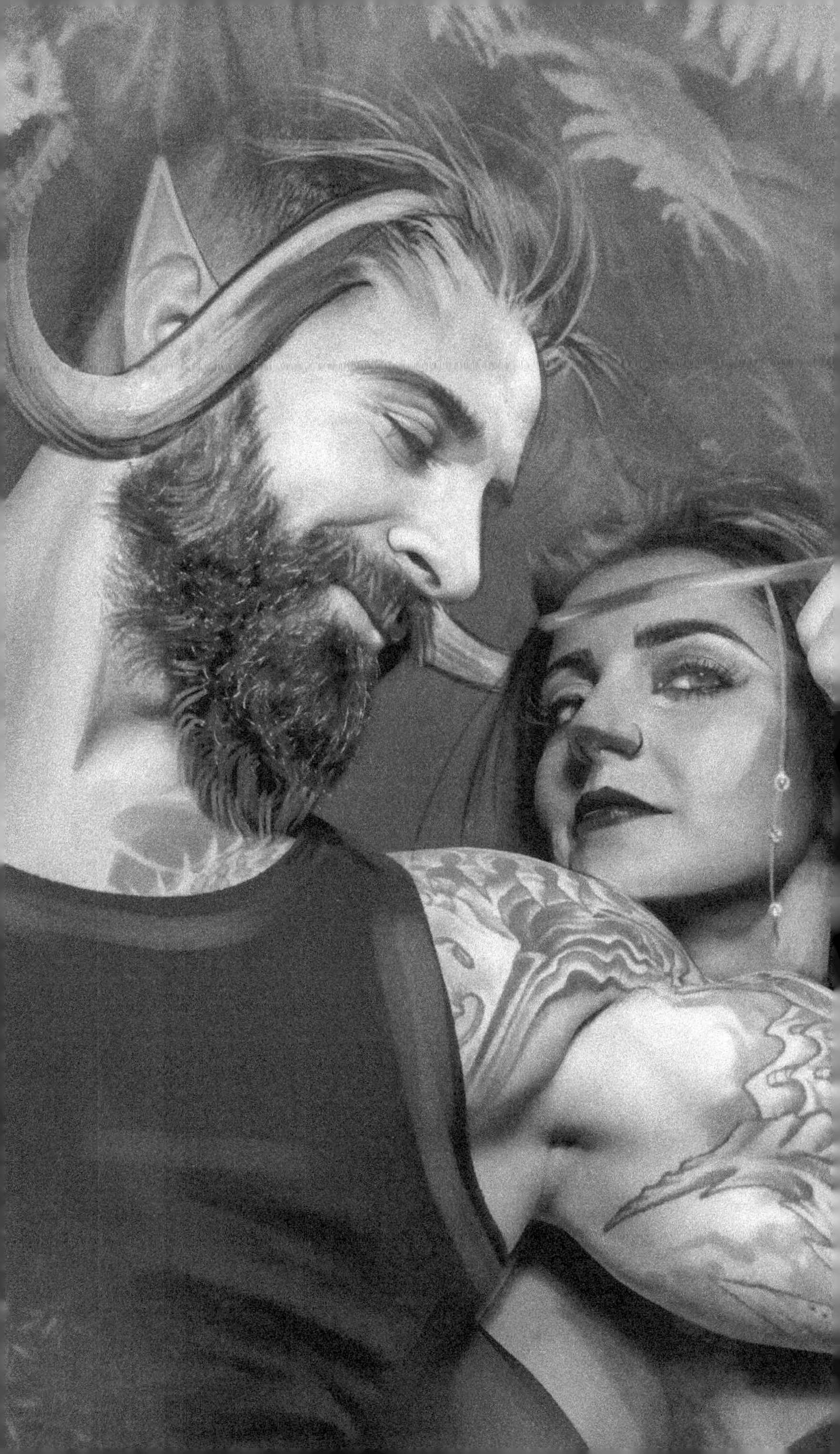

CHAPTER 5

Anise stood dumbly as she watched Caraway's big, leather-clad body disappear down into the gully.

The baby cried again, and it sliced right through her heart. She hadn't expected Caraway to return to the troll. The shock of it still atrophied her muscles.

Caraway—getting involved in the plight of others, even when it seemingly had nothing to do with his job. This went against everything he stood for, or rather, everything the Order of the Well stood for.

Maybe the Order *was* changing. Maybe the world was.

The frozen, harsh landscape that had taught the fae to be so brutal and ruthless was decreasing. The world was getting bigger once more.

Anise blinked and looked down at the portal stone. It was her ticket to seeing the Ice-Witch, to garner the

ability to shift and hold mana, but it had been left in the safekeeping of a child-eating Unseelie troll who wore trophies of his kills around his neck. She wanted to hurl the stone into the sky and forget about her journey, but a small part of her reasoned away this knowledge.

Maybe the Ice-Witch didn't know the troll was like this. Maybe she did.

Did it matter?

If Anise acquired the ability to shift, then did it matter who helped her get it?

Anise knew the witch was Unseelie. She knew the morally obtuse woman would have different methods, and that was precisely why Anise was going to see her. No fae in Seelie territory offered the ability to grant changes to her physical makeup. Dark magic was the only way to inject chaos into creation, and the Unseelie had no compunction when it came to dealing with the inky side of the Well.

The baby's cry pricked her ears forward and goosebumps erupted over her skin. Whatever Anise thought of the witch, there were more important things to do right now. She pocketed the stone, unsheathed her dagger, and jogged after Caraway.

When she arrived at the cave, her heart leaped into her throat. The troll's head was on the floor—separate from his body—and Caraway stood with his broadsword to his side, its tip bloody and scraping the ground as he stalked closer to something beyond the campfire at the mouth of

the cave. She'd never seen that kind of fury in his expression. He was formidable.

Caraway stopped. The campfire blocked him from his quarry.

Anise could tell he was calculating how to approach the situation. The tension in his shoulders pulled tight. The tips of his horns quivered. And an unearthly breeze gusted his hair, as though the mana he held ripe within his body, ready for hostile release, was quivering to get out. It just needed a target.

Anise crept up behind him and almost lost the contents of her stomach when she saw what was in the cave beyond the fire. Another troll, this one bigger and fatter. The orange firelight cast sinister shadows along its craggy body. It cradled the wailing baby in its arms and held it to the side as if it were protecting the baby, but Anise knew it was the opposite. The troll inched toward the campfire near the cave mouth and snarled, the evidence of its last meal dangled between its teeth.

She palmed the hilt of her dagger. If either her or Caraway struck the troll, the baby would fall. Whatever they decided, they must act fast before the baby ended up in the fire.

Caraway frowned at Anise. "I told you to stay put."

"When do I ever do what I'm told?" She edged up to his side and whispered, "What do we do?"

"I can't strike and cast a spell at the same time. I'm not that good."

"But I can strike," she replied. "Be ready to catch the baby."

"Anise," Caraway warned, but she'd already taken a step closer.

She threw her dagger at the troll's face and wished it to land true. Its blade whistled past the flames and sunk into the troll's eye. It let loose an almighty roar and released the baby so it could pull the dagger free.

Panic choked Anise at the sight of the falling baby. She was already halfway around the fire as the troll stumbled backward, but Caraway beat her. He hadn't taken a step, yet the baby hovered in mid-air. He'd cast some kind of air-hardening spell around it to keep it safe.

She'd never been more relieved to have a Guardian as a friend, and even more so that he'd insisted on coming on this journey. If he'd not, she'd never have been able to rescue this baby on her own. It would have ended another trophy around the trolls' necks. She found a fluffy blanket on the straw mattress and swaddled the baby before gathering it into her arms. Then she quickly got as far into the gully as she could to avoid the smoke.

"It's all right, little one," she crooned. "We've got you."

Anise washed the baby's red face and gave it something to drink from a waterskin she'd had in her bag.

Caraway came back, blood dripping from his sword in one hand, and her soiled dagger in his other.

"Is it okay?" His deep voice cracked with concern.

She nodded. "For now, but we need to get it—" she

took a peek inside the blanket. "Him. It's a boy." She gulped a deep breath. "No fur on his ears. No wings. How will we know which fae race he belongs to, or where to take him?"

"We take him to the Order."

Anise winced. "But you went against Order rules." Her watering eyes locked with her friend's. "Why?"

Why, when he'd always avoided getting involved in the past?

He held her stare.

"Maybe what happened to you has taught me some things. Maybe right or wrong doesn't have defined borders." He shrugged. "You were right, Anise. If I've got the ability to do something, I should."

The smile she sent him stretched so wide it hurt her cheeks. "Good to see something is getting through that woolly head of yours."

Their moment didn't last long before she saw something flicker in his eyes. Consequence. He may be finally understanding that saving all lives matters, but nothing happened in a vacuum. Caraway's actions could have dire consequences, and if his convictions weren't strong enough, then he'd ultimately blame her for any punishment he received as a result of saving this baby.

The Guardians took following orders seriously, and if you failed, you weren't much use to the Order.

Her smile faded. "I hope you didn't do this just to make me happy."

"I thought this is what you wanted? Me getting involved."

Turmoil swirled in her stomach. "I want you to get involved with things like this because it's the right thing to do, not because you think it would make me happy."

The baby started crying again, and Anise tucked it close.

"We can finish this conversation later," he said and pulled out a portal stone from his pocket. "For now, we'd better get the infant to safety. This is the only stone I have keyed to the Order, but I can get another while we're there. Unless you had an alternative route back from the Ice-Witch."

She shrugged. She had planned to shift into a wolf form and use her more weather-proof animal body to trot home. Wolves could travel miles through the snow in one day. Failure hadn't been an option. But now... now she understood things could go wrong.

Caraway's boss, the Prime, might let him off with a wrist slap for what he'd done, but if Anise let him follow her to the Ice-Witch, and he got into more trouble, she wouldn't forgive herself. This rebellion thing of his was new to him, despite herself harping on about it for years. He needed time to process his actions and motivations. Anise refused to be the one who ruined the life he'd built for himself, not when he'd struggled after leaving his pacifist family behind for the violent life at the Order.

When they arrived at the Order, she would find

someone to activate the portal stone to the Ice-Witch, and she would leave Caraway behind. It was the right choice.

⚖

When they arrived in the field outside the Order of the Well compound, Anise handed the baby to Caraway.

"I'll wait for you here," she said.

He frowned. "Are you sure? Clarke is probably inside."

As tempting as it was to see her friend, Anise already felt her resolve weakening, and visiting the Ice-Witch had been her sole purpose for half a decade. She couldn't chicken out now.

"I'm good," she said.

He raised a brow, but turned and left. When the big compound gates closed after he'd walked through, she turned and pulled out the troll's portal stone from her pocket. The smooth, warm surface fit in the palm of her hand. She assumed there would be a magical reaction when she touched it—if she held mana within her body. She wondered what it would feel like to be connected viscerally to all the magic in the world, to have her own internal Well that fed from the grand Cosmic Well.

But she didn't.

And it was because she didn't that Caraway had already gotten into trouble. The Prime wouldn't be happy about his meddling, let alone bringing home a stray baby. And if he kept assisting in Anise's journey to the witch, then she would feel the same as she always did—useless.

The stone could be another test. The Ice-Witch knew why Anise sought her out. She'd have known that Anise couldn't activate a portal stone on her own, that she'd need help.

If Caraway hadn't been there, she'd probably have had to barter with the troll to get him to activate it, or to travel to a village and find a high fae to help her.

With a sigh, she faced the guard on top of the wall surrounding the Order compound. He wore a helmet made from hardened leather and a black leather Guardian uniform. A longbow was in his hands, and a quiver of arrows strapped to his back.

"Excuse me," she said, waving up to him.

He looked down.

"I'm running late for my appointment. Would you mind terribly if you activated my portal stone for me? I'm afraid I'm not as strong as you and lack your power."

When in doubt, she always found a well-timed ego-stroking compliment worked. He blinked, glanced over his shoulder to the other side of the wall, and then nodded.

"Toss it up."

Trying not to hide her smile, she threw it. He caught it deftly and pointed to where he was going to activate the portal. Within moments, a bright light tore a slice through the fabric of space. The light grew in size until it became a giant circle, her destination showing through the middle in a brightly blurred scene of snow and ice.

This was it.

Her heart pounded. She experienced a flicker of doubt at leaving her friend, but knew it was for the best. If she couldn't even see the Ice-Witch on her own, then what was the point of going on this quest?

She tossed a grateful smile at the guard, and then walked through the portal.

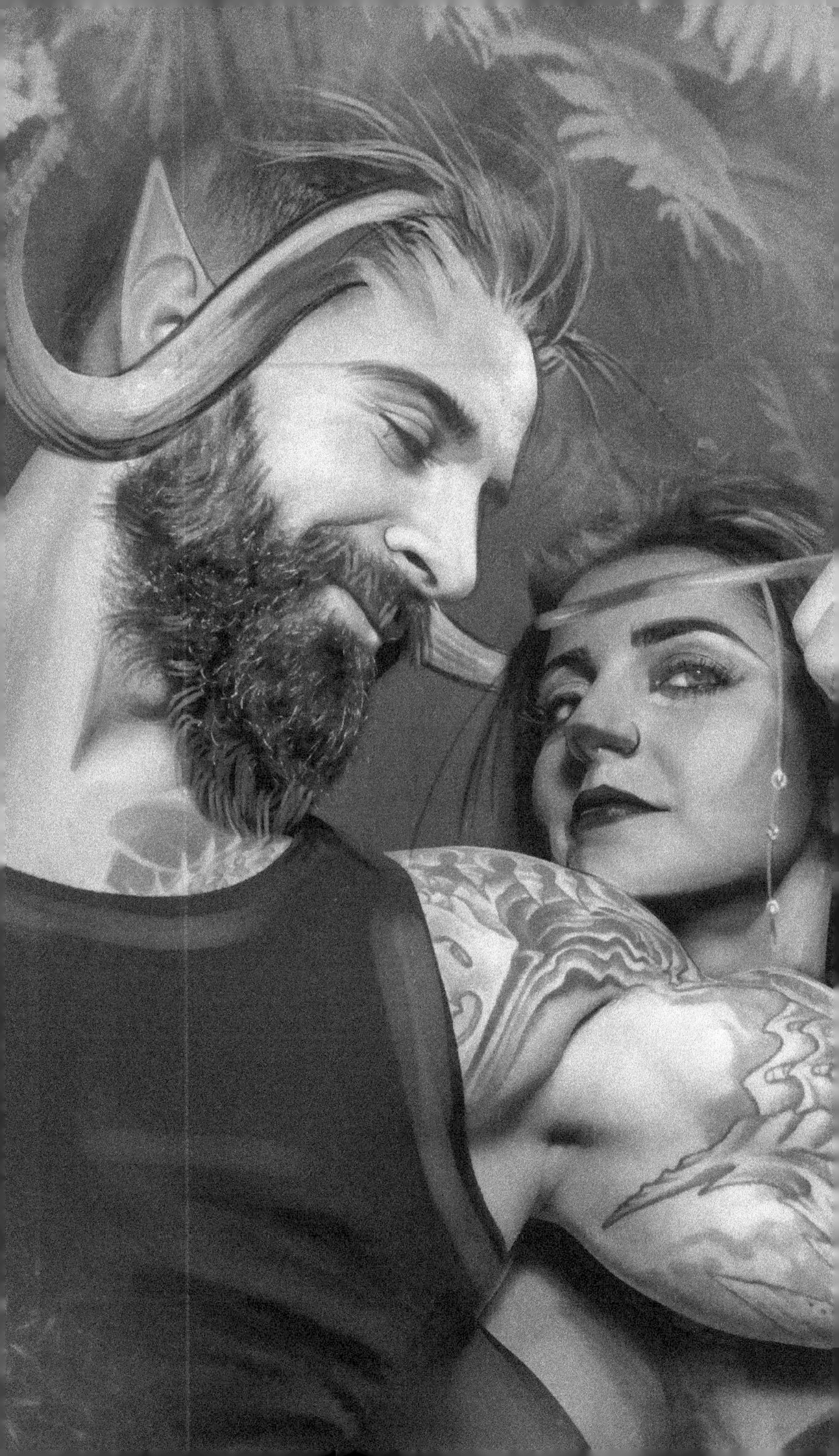

CHAPTER 6

After leaving the child with a Mage, Caraway returned to the gate with an incorrigible smile on his face. Even the Prime's tongue-lashing about working outside the scope of his station hadn't ruffled his fur. He'd done something that felt good.

Because of him, this child would have the chance to grow up.

This was why he'd left his family in the first place—to save those who couldn't save themselves. It was why he became a Guardian. He couldn't believe he'd forgotten that, despite Anise's urging to do so. Some part of him must have still been locked into an old way of thinking, one where he could only do his job if he colored inside the lines. But life wasn't ordered. It was chaotic.

"Violence begets violence," his mother had once said.

"Violence protects. It teaches your enemy to be afraid of you."

"Well, congratulations, son. We are now afraid of you."

He shoved the memories down and focused on the one shining light in his life. Anise. He couldn't wait to tell her what he'd said when the Prime had tried to block him from leaving. He'd told her that if she wanted to keep him as a Guardian, then she'd better get used to him stepping in to help those unfortunate, whether it was Well-related or not. He'd said the Order needed this kind of image boost after the Prime's totalitarian ways, and then he didn't stop to wait for the Prime's response.

Coming up to the gate, he gestured for the guard on top to open it and let him out. When he emerged into the field outside the Order compound, he couldn't find Anise. At first, he thought perhaps she'd gone inside after all, but he'd barely spent time at the Academy where he'd flagged down a healing Mage. The Prime had accosted him on the way back out. If Anise had entered the compound, she'd have walked straight past him.

He lifted his gaze to the sentry's post and squinted into the sun.

"Where did the female go?" he asked.

The guard shrugged. "Somewhere snowy, I guess."

Caraway's heart clenched. "What do you mean?"

"She asked me to activate her portal stone. Said she couldn't do it."

No.

Caraway shook his head, refusing to believe it. She wouldn't leave without him, would she? He'd felt like they

were finally connecting again. But she had left. Not only had she entered dangerous territory on her own, but she was still planning on going through with her quest for the ability to shift. No bargain made with the Ice-Witch would be safe. And then there was the mission part of his reason for following her. Caraway might not agree with the Prime's way of leading sometimes, but he stood behind the Order's mission to keep magic alive in Elphyne. They needed to know whether the Ice-Witch was responsible for supplying the human enemy with mana-warped monsters.

Mild panic swarmed his skin like prickling ant bites. He had to get Leaf. Without preamble, he headed back into the Order to find the Cadre of Twelve's team leader, and resident expert at tracing portals.

⚖

CARAWAY STOOD behind Leaf and Aeron as they assessed the space in the air where Anise's portal had been activated. Leaf glared at the space with glowing blue eyes. It seemed as if he saw through the air to another dimension. His compatriot, Aeron, also looked at something Caraway couldn't see.

They were tracing the portal—tracking where it had sent Anise.

Both elves were adept at casting spells with their inherent mana. As far as Caraway knew, there was no one more skilled than Leaf. He shuddered to think how

powerful Leaf would become if he gained a Well-blessed mate like his cadre members, Rush and Thorne.

Aeron's braided brown hair swung down his spine every time he nodded to Leaf with another increment of portal remnant he assessed.

Caraway could see none of it.

This skill took decades, possibly centuries, to hone. It was why these two were part of the cadre, the Order's most elite warriors, and not Caraway.

"I've almost got it," Leaf murmured. Small droplets of perspiration dotted the skin over his smooth top lip.

"She's far north-west," Aeron added. "In the cold."

Leaf made a swiping motion with his hand, and a tearing sound ripped through the air. He reopened the portal and turned to Caraway, "I hope she brought a woolen cape."

Caraway gave a curt nod. He didn't need one. Being a muskox-shifter, and one of the fire-fae, his temperature ran hot.

Aeron put something smooth into Caraway's palm. When Caraway looked down, he found another portal stone. But he'd already taken one from the Mage Academy. He raised a brow at Aeron.

"It's from Clarke. It's keyed to Rush's cabin."

"Why?" Caraway asked. Clarke was psychic. Had she seen some reason that he'd be needing to take a detour home?

Aeron shrugged. "Who knows with Clarke? I'm

guessing she'll want to meet you there before you come here."

Caraway nodded his gratitude, braced, and then headed through the portal.

Leaf reminded Caraway as he left, "Just reconnaissance."

⚖

THE ICE-FOREST WAS APTLY NAMED for the trees of frozen water. Clear crystalline trunks four hand-spans wide stretched high into the blue sky. Icicle leaves swayed and tinkled with the arctic breeze as Caraway navigated the only path available. The portal had taken him to the brink of the forest. It was either head backward over a vast icy tundra, or deep into the forest. It made sense the Ice-Witch would live in a frozen forest—he hoped—and not the barren tundra.

But the further he trekked, the more doubt crept into his mind. Every few hundred feet, he picked up a new worrying sign that things weren't going according to Anise's plan.

Specks of blood were stark against the ice. At first, the drops looked like they'd come from a scratch, or a shallow wound, but then he came to a place in the path where ice had chipped away from trunks, the ground was littered with fallen icicle leaves, and the tiny red droplets arced in a line as though someone had been cut and blood had spurted. With each passing minute, he stared at the blood

spatter, his chest constricted painfully until it felt like his ribcage squashed his heart.

Anise *had* to be okay.

He wouldn't accept another outcome.

A screech shook the leaves and a shower of ice rained down on Caraway's head. He released Reckoning and crouched into a battle stance, ears straining, and eyes searching the sky. A light shadow blocked the sun. Then another, and another. Screeching grew in timbre. More powdered ice dropped from the trees.

What's up there?

Air trembled.

Crushed shards of leaves fell to the ground, hitting his shoulders.

Glamor was a common tool in the fae arsenal, and whatever hunted him could be using it to hide from sight. Then again, it could also be a camouflage system of the beasts. Caraway closed his eyes and focused on senses other than sight. He let the air enter his lungs, held, and then exhaled slowly. Through it all, his ears strained and he sent out a blanket of magic to surround him. Whether it was his pacifist roots or something the Well had gifted him during his initiation ceremony, Caraway had learned that as a Guardian, he excelled in protective spells, including casting forcefields around his body—or the baby he'd saved.

Any being entering his immediate surroundings would trigger his alarm system, and he'd know where to strike.

All he had to do was wait.

So he breathed, and he listened, and he sensed. Like trying to catch a fish, he waited for a thrumming ping down the line he'd cast.

Ping.

He spun and thrust Reckoning into a solid ice wall. An ear-piercing shriek rattled his bones, and a crashing sound like breaking glass followed. When he opened his eyes, he paused from the sheer shock of what he saw. A broken sculpture of a gargoyle made from ice, not stone. But he could've sworn it had been moving through the air, rattling the leaves of the trees enough to shatter them.

Caraway nudged the large broken chunks of solid ice with his sword. No blood, just a clear crystalline body through and through. If he'd needed any evidence the witch was creating mana-warped monsters, this could be it. Except... the ice would melt soon, and there would be nothing left. He needed more.

The ice also meant the blood he'd seen on the way had indeed belonged to Anise.

He was still lost in thought when he heard another screech, only then remembering that he'd heard more than one creature calling earlier. A thud behind him had him tensing. He gripped the hilt of his sword painfully. A bloom of white breath ghosted over his shoulder. He whirled, ready to strike, and came face to face with another angry ice-gargoyle. It opened its jaws, screeched again. Its white breath turned putrid and green.

Was it... poison?

Dark spots swam before his eyes. He tried to swing at

the beast, knowing the magic-nulling properties of his sword would help, but staggered like a drunk to the floor where everything went dark.

Too late.

His last thought was of Anise's sassy smile.

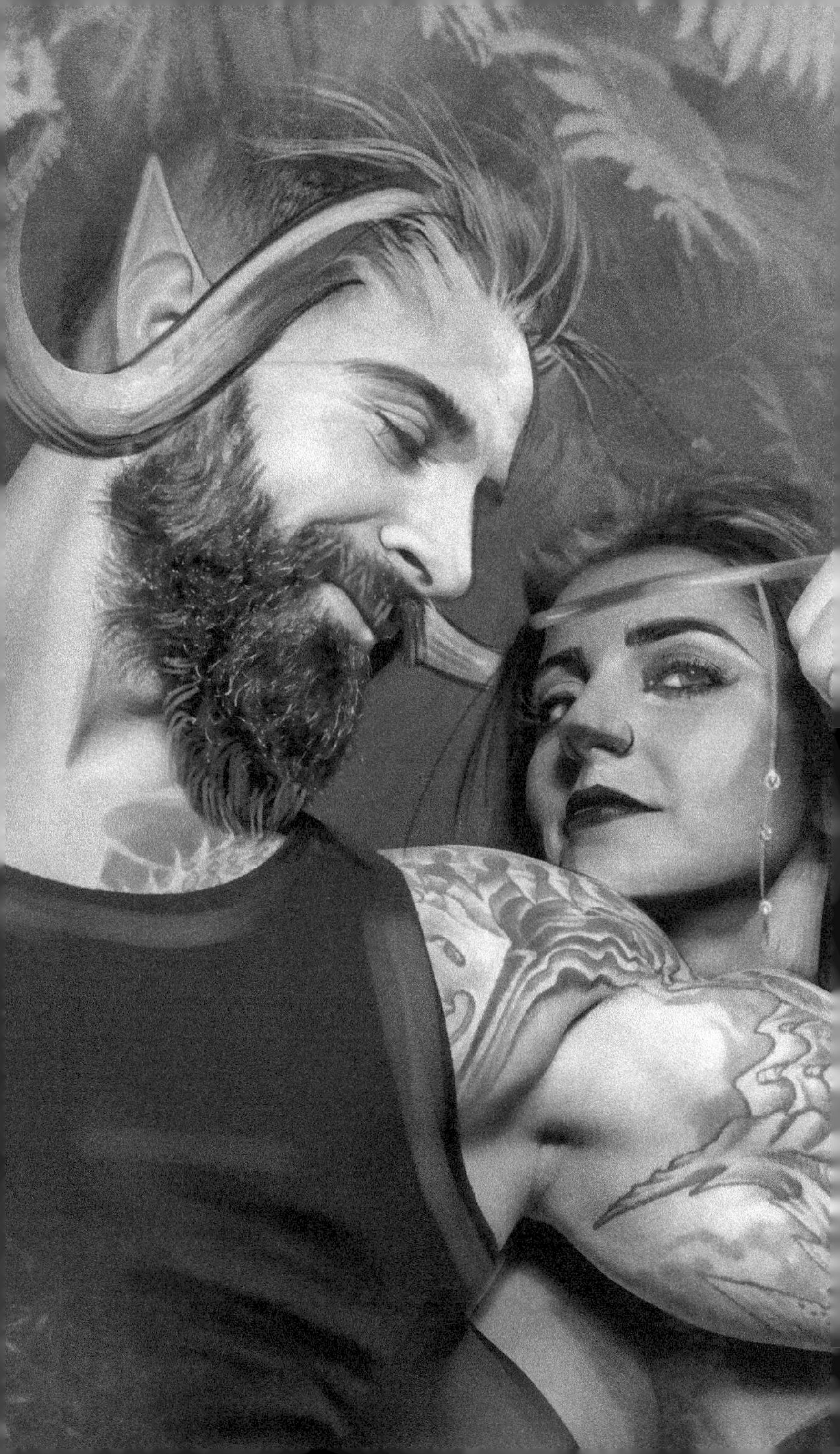

CHAPTER 7

Their prison was a domed room made of solid snow. Light came from the only exit, guarded by two winged beasts carved from ice. There was no water, no food, and no toilet.

Anise gently patted Caraway's cheek but he didn't stir.

Crimson, when those frozen beasts had dragged his lifeless body in, she'd felt sick. It still hadn't returned to normal. He had to wake soon. *He had to!*

She patted his cheek again. No reaction. But at least he was warm and breathed evenly.

In an attempt to calm herself, Anise shifted her position so she could sit against the solid snow wall and lifted Caraway's big head into her lap. It felt better to hold him.

He moaned. She let her knuckles graze his cheek and then rasp over the scruff on his jaw. She'd always fantasized about touching him... his face, his jaw, his horns. But the horns weren't there this time. He was a shifter, so

perhaps he'd morphed them away. She'd just never seen him do that in all the years she'd known him.

It wouldn't surprise her if he'd chosen to keep his horns visible when he didn't have to. Usually, a shifters' natural fae-form was close to human, with only arched ears as a sign they were *other*, touched by the magic of the Well, but never Caraway. He'd always had his curved lethal horns proudly jutting from his head. He'd probably left them there to look as far from human as he could.

Humans were manaless, untouched, greedy leeches that constantly tried to invade Elphyne and reap the benefits of the Well, yet refused to follow the rules that provided Well's magic in the first place.

No metal. No plastic. Two simple rules.

But the humans had run out of metals in their city. They'd come raiding in Elphyne to look for places to mine for resources.

Caraway's peace-loving family were victims of one such raid. As nomads, they'd lived amongst the western snowy tundra. A human-led raiding party had massacred half his tribe. His family's answer was to migrate further inland. Caraway's answer was to join the Guardians where he gained enhanced powers to help him hunt humans and return the favor.

Anise's home town, Crescent Hollow, was the closest fae settlement to the human city. Because of this proximity, Caraway was always there, sitting in the tavern where Anise had worked. Sometimes before a hunt, sometimes

after, but every time he spoke of the race that murdered his kinsfolk, his cheeks would redden with fury.

"That's what I like about you folk here in Crescent Hollow," he'd once said. *"You're so far from human even though you're so close. You never forget what it means to be fae."*

Crescent Hollow was a wolf-shifter town. But Anise couldn't shift.

"Without your tail and ears, you're basically human!"

The cruel taunts of her childhood still haunted her. She couldn't be the thing that Caraway hated. She had to stand on her own two feet and hold her own the way mana-filled fae could.

Caraway stirred again.

Long lashes lifted slowly, warily. Warm brown eyes focused on her and then widened.

"You're okay," he said, incredulously. "But I saw blood."

She smiled gently and showed her healing forearm. "I cut myself on one of those ice beasts, but I had some elven healing cream in my bag. I've stopped bleeding now."

He blinked, seemingly processing her words. Then he sat up sharply and enveloped her smaller body within his. The force of his strong arms locked around her. She stiffened on reflex until his hold tightened, and then she melted into him.

For long, silent minutes, they held each other and the world was right.

It was just the two of them, warm bodies fused together in an icy world. Why couldn't life be this simple?

Caraway pulled back just enough that he could look down into her eyes.

"Anise," he said, voice deep and rough. "I thought I'd lost you."

"I'm here," she replied.

Charged awareness bounced between them. They were close. So Well-damned close that she could stick out her tongue and lick his lips. *Crimson*, she wanted to. They'd never been in an embrace like this, and they both knew it.

How would he react? Would he pull away and act as many others did?

What are you dumb as well as less? The voice of her last customer rang through her mind. Her heart sank. She lowered her eyes, but Caraway used his finger to tilt her chin up. This time, there was an intensity in his gaze that rocked her to her core. Heat and desire stirred in her lower belly. Confused, she frowned at him.

His intensity held until she squirmed. Then he licked his lips, looked down at hers, and leaned in until there was no doubt in her mind what he was about to do. She froze with anticipation. Her nerves thrummed with energy.

The tips of their noses touched and his lashes shuttered as though he was in pain. Their breaths came in stilted gasps… and then he moved his lips an iota. *Closer*.

They didn't kiss. Not yet. Maybe he was thinking the same things as she—that this kiss would change everything. That this was the one thing she'd always wanted,

but feared would never happen. That he would turn away and change his mind. That she was less, and not good enough.

But he nudged his lips toward hers. He closed the gap. He lifted her chin. *Almost.*

And then... soft lips landed on hers, capturing her mouth, leaving her breathless. She went liquid with a moan.

Caraway growled with approval, splayed a big hand at her back, and tugged her closer as though she weighed nothing to him. Damn, he was strong. It sent a thrill tripping through her stomach. Her soft front slammed against his hard chest and he deepened their kiss.

Yes. He wanted this too.

Knowing it flipped a switch inside her. She speared fingers into his hair, tightened her grip, kissed harder, and drank him up. Her tongue dueled with his and plundered his mouth for more. His taste was like a drug, and he must have felt the same way because he held her so tight she could barely move. When they finally broke for air, they still couldn't let go of each other.

He felt hot, hard, a little sweaty, and she wanted more.

"Anise," he rasped deeply, eyes searching hers. Something flickered in them, and her doubt came hurtling back.

He's going to say this is a mistake.

Before he could speak, she blurted the first thing that came to mind. "Your horns are gone. I've never seen you without them."

He blinked. His jaw clicked shut. And he frowned. "What?"

She gestured to his head.

Caraway's looming body pulled back. His warmth went with him.

"So stupid. I forgot," he admonished himself.

The air shimmered around his head, and then two sharp horns grew from above his temples until they curved down and outward from his cheekbones.

The shame in his posture surprised Anise. His eyes turned downcast.

"It's because you think you look human without the horns, don't you?" she asked, and then elaborated. "You keep the horns so you look different to those who killed your family."

He jerked back. "Why would you think that?"

"I don't know. I guess you're always talking about how much you hate them, and how much you love the shifters at Crescent Hollow looking so different to them."

His brows lowered. His gaze darkened. "Anise, I don't love the shifters at the Hollow because they *look* different from humans. They *are* different from humans. Especially you—you're kind, selfless, and brave." He shuffled closer and lifted her chin to look hard into her eyes. "I keep my horns because you're self-conscious of your tail. I do it so you think we're the same outside and in—" He tapped her sternum. "From the moment I met you, Anise, you've accepted me for who I am. Unlike my family, who disowned me for wanting to protect them, you've always

taken me as I came. I keep my horns to show you I accept you as you are."

Anise's mind whirled with his confession.

He kept his horns so she didn't feel left out. So she felt less alone. He thought she was kind, selfless, and brave.

Her fingers wrapped around the smooth length of his horns and tugged until his lips came back to hers. This time, there was no hesitation. The two of them kissed as though their hearts pulled their puppet strings, directing them with passion, desire, and need. They were so lost in each other, they failed to notice their companion until she spoke.

"This is so sweet I'm getting cavities."

They broke apart. Caraway shoved Anise behind him and bared his teeth at the intruder.

The Ice-Witch was here, and she wasn't anything like the hag Anise had expected.

A tall, willowy female fae leaned with her shoulder against the doorway. White ringlets bounced around a pale, heart-shaped face. She had a dusky nose, flushed cheeks, and white rabbit ears that poked through an orange top hat and pointed straight up. Her outfit was a mix of black, white, and orange lace and wool. A corset squeezed abundant breasts out the top, and slick black woolen pants revealed a twitching bunny rabbit tail at the rear. When she smiled, two large front teeth touched her bottom lip.

She shifted red eyes to Anise. "I'm ready to see you now."

When Anise moved, Caraway held her back.

The witch clicked her tongue. "Now, now, Guardian. Is that any way to behave?"

"Don't make the deal, Anise," he said over his shoulder. "You don't need to change. You're perfect the way you are."

All humor in the witch's face flatlined. She glared at Caraway. "You don't get a say in her choice when you haven't been honest about your true reason for being here."

Anise stiffened and locked on Caraway. "What's she talking about?"

Guilt flashed over his features.

"Caraway?" she prompted.

"I'm here on a mission," he admitted. "For the Order."

She stepped away from him, shocked. So... he wasn't here to support her? It had been a ruse?

"Anise," he reached for her, but she stepped further back and he flinched. "It doesn't change the fact I don't want you to make a bargain with this female. Please don't. I'm begging you."

"All this time," she said, "I thought maybe you actually missed me. That's why you came to see me after two years, but it wasn't. You're only using me to get to the Ice-Witch, aren't you?"

His lack of an answer was all she needed to know.

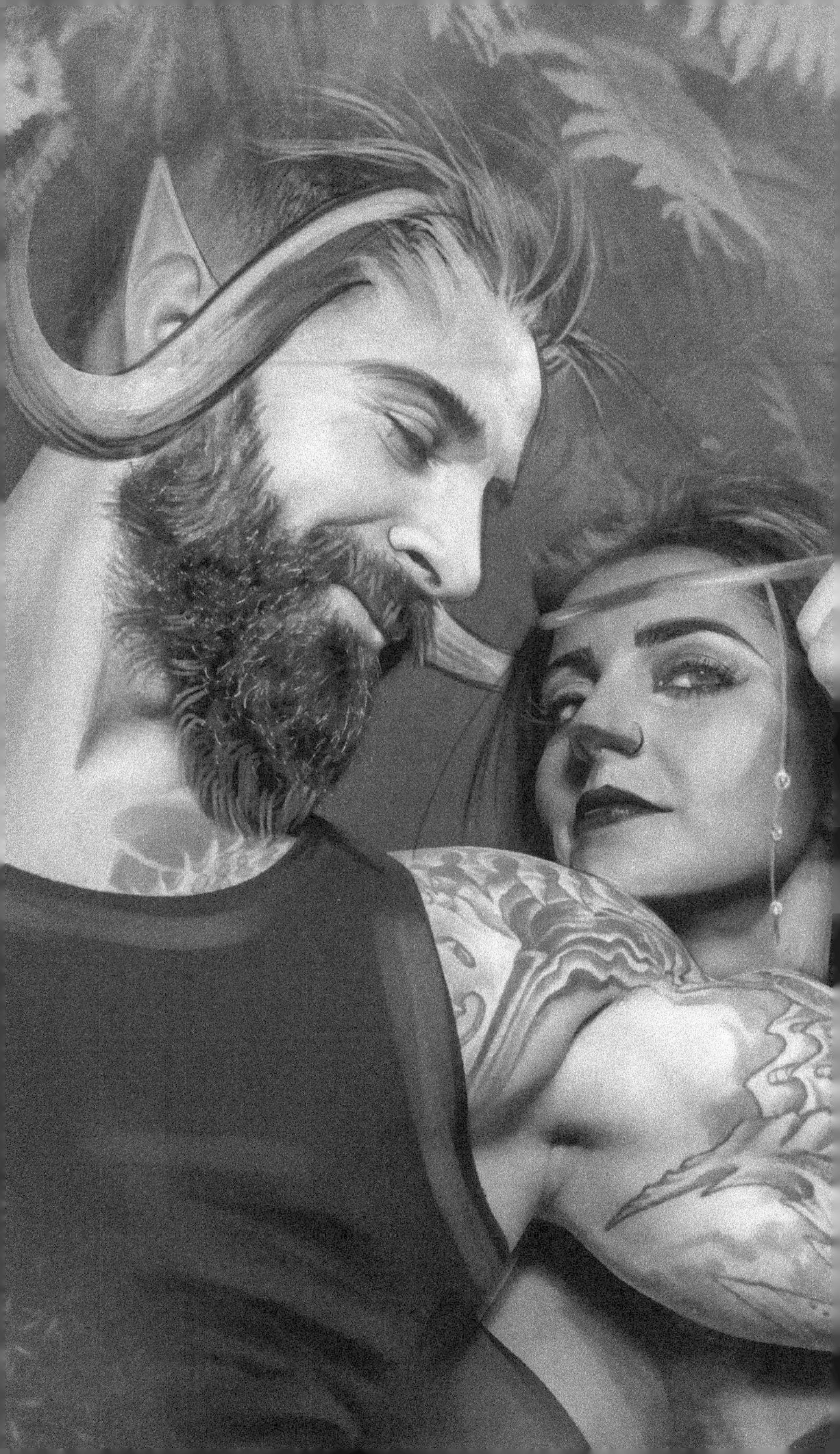

CHAPTER 8

Caraway roared his anger at the ice-gargoyles from his prison, but the two beasts blocked him solidly. There was no way through.

The witch had taken Anise away before he could explain, *before he could say sorry*.

He punched the snowy wall until shards of stalactite ice dropped from the ceiling. One was so sharp, it cut the back of his hand as it came down. He landed heavily on the ground and dipped his head into his hands.

Damn him.

He should have been honest with Anise from the start. She would have understood, surely. Now he was stuck in an icy prison while his love was about to make the biggest mistake of her life.

He needed his sword, and he needed it now.

The gargoyles were magical creatures. They wouldn't have touched Reckoning for fear of it affecting them-

selves. It was probably rusting on the path where he'd been poisoned.

Caraway's head lifted.

A slow smile formed as a plan came to mind. Recently, Thorne had shown him a handy little trick. As one of the Cadre of Twelve, and Well-blessed to boot, Thorne was more adept at spell casting than Caraway could ever hope to be. The wolf-shifter had been recently imprisoned in the Ring—a gladiator type pit where differences were decided through a battle to the death. He'd been thrown in without his weapon, but years earlier he'd carved a transference rune onto his battle-ax's handle. When he was in the Ring, all he'd needed to do was scratch that same rune onto his palm, and the spell would hunt down the weapon and bring it to him. Thorne had single-handedly won a battle against multiple mana-warped creatures because he'd had the might of his magic-cutting ax.

After hearing the story, Caraway had immediately carved a transference rune into Reckoning's handle. Collecting a broken shard of stalactite, Caraway carved the rune into his palm and activated the spell, then he positioned himself behind the gargoyles and waited. A whooshing sound came, the air twisted and heated, and then Caraway felt a solid familiar weight land in the palm of his right hand.

Reckoning.

He grinned.

Anise followed the witch through a long hallway carved from clear ice. While the witch didn't seem to feel the cold, Anise felt it through to her bones. She hugged her cape around her shoulders and forced her teeth to stop chattering.

It wasn't only her skin that was numb, but her heart and mind. She couldn't comprehend Caraway had only followed her on this quest to use her. Did she know him at all? It hurt to think it was all a manipulation.

Her heart didn't want to believe it. His kiss had been real. He couldn't fake that.

I keep my horns to show you I accept you as you are.

Anise's chest constricted. Her eyes watered.

"Here we go," the witch's sickly sweet voice echoed.

Anise looked up and found they'd emerged into a large hall. Like the rest of this part of the world, it was all made from ice. Cobwebs hung from the ceiling like a sick sort of decoration. Prismatic light filtered through the ceiling from outside, making Anise realize it must still be day. As she followed the witch, Anise noticed strange shadows encased in the ice walls. The closer she got, the more she wanted to vomit.

The shadows were people, frozen with terror on their faces. Were they others like Anise, who'd come looking for answers, or were they fae who'd done the witch wrong?

Anise hugged her cape tighter.

The witch took steps up to a podium where an ice-

throne sat. She sprawled into the seat and crooked her finger at Anise.

"Come closer, dear."

Anise shuffled forward but stopped at the foot of the dais. "Where's my bone dagger?" she asked.

"You'll get it when you leave." The witch slipped out the dagger from her boot and stabbed it into the arm of her throne. The hilt wobbled as it took purchase. "I couldn't very well leave intruders in my home with weapons, could I?"

"Intruder?" Anise gasped. "I was invited."

"The Guardian was not."

"Nor was he excluded."

The witch's gaze narrowed on Anise. "He killed my troll."

Anise tried not to let her panic show on her face. She had also killed a troll, and no matter what Caraway had done to get into this place, she didn't want him to die for it. And she would never regret saving that baby's life.

"What are you going to do with Caraway?" she asked.

"Well, now. That depends on you."

Anise took a step back. "What do you mean?"

"Well, my dear. How are you planning to pay for the ability to shift?"

"I have coin. Lots of it. That's how I plan to pay."

The witch laughed. It was a high-pitched melodious tinkle. "What makes you think I need coin?"

"Then what do you want?"

"Two hundred years," she stated and then gestured to

the poor souls trapped in the ice. "After two hundred years, you pay me with a soul."

Anise bit her lip. "But I get the power of a shifter for two hundred years?"

She could live as one of the wolves in Crescent Hollow for two centuries before she needed to lose her soul. And in that time, she could shift into a wolf, run through the forest, and feel the joy and freedom other shifters always waxed poetic about when they'd come into the tavern. For two centuries, she would hold mana within her body and cast spells without needing to resort to potions or elixirs. Wasn't that all she'd wanted? To belong?

"You don't need to change. You're perfect the way you are."

Part of her wanted to believe Caraway's words, and part of her wanted to not need to. She hated that she yearned for his approval, the same as everyone else's. She hated that she wanted to fit in, but the constant anxiety was a noose over her head. She'd never be rid of it if she didn't try this.

The witch squinted at her. "I can see you have doubts, and I know it's because of the male who followed you. Let me give you a piece of free advice." She leaned forward in her throne until her orange top hat tilted on her head. If it weren't for her rabbit ears poking through cutout holes, the hat may have fallen right off. "Males, of any species, are not to be trusted. They take what they want, but they'll never give you what you need. It's in their nature. They're the hunters, not the nurturers. The sooner you come to terms with that, the better."

That's when Anise realized every frozen body in the ice was male.

The witch stood and stepped down the dais. With wistful eyes, she trailed her fingers along the icy walls of her macabre museum.

"I wasn't always like this." She gestured to her ears. "I used to shift into a rabbit. And like you, I came looking for a way to become more than less. But then I found him." She stopped at a particular shadowed figure trapped in the ice. A tall fae, handsome and ominous in his expression, even as he was petrified. "He seduced me, and he stole my mana. He harvested it for his own use. But you see, he made a mistake. He believed that those lesser fae were beneath him." She snarled at the shadow. "He should have killed me when he had the chance."

"Caraway's stolen nothing from me," Anise said. Her experience wasn't the same as this female's.

The witch's eyes snapped toward Anise. "All males are the same."

Anise shook her head. Perhaps the witch's story was meant to convince her to give up on Caraway, but it only made her realize he wasn't Anise's enemy. He'd never believed she was beneath him. No, she loved him. She wouldn't involve him in this.

"I just want the ability to shift."

The witch held out her hand. "So we have a deal?"

Anise paused, but two hundred years of fulfillment was a long time. She could be happy.

She nodded and shook the witch's hand. "Yes, we have a deal."

Thunder cracked through the hall. The walls shook. Tiny icicles showered from the ceiling. Anise thought, perhaps, that it was because of the bargain they'd just struck, but the witch's facial expression was as surprised as Anise's.

They disengaged and Anise repeated. "You give me the ability to shift into a wolf for two hundred years, and I give you my soul after that."

"Oh, little wolf. It's too late to add specifics." The witch's peach lips curved into a wicked grin. "Now, I didn't say *whose* soul was payment."

Then she laughed a big cackling sound that shriveled Anise's resolve. What could she mean? Not Anise's soul? Then whose—

Caraway burst into the room, his face contorted in fury, his fist around his long broadsword. Long legs strode into the center of the hall.

"What did you do?" he demanded to the witch.

He stormed toward where she had retreated to her throne. He raised his sword high above his head, but before he could arc his swing downward, the witch flicked her wrist and ice shot out of the ground beneath his feet. Water sprung like a geyser to surround Caraway's body. It only took seconds, and his sword was knocked from his hands. It clattered loudly to the ground.

"No!" Anise shouted. "Leave him alone."

But the witch just laughed as the water slithered up

Caraway's body and turned to ice. His doe-eyed gaze flicked to Anise, and then to his fallen sword with a forlorn finality before he became completely encased—frozen.

Anise hissed at the witch. "No! I don't agree to give him. Let him go."

The witch clicked her tongue and then pouted. "Yes, you did agree."

"He's not mine to give," Anise insisted.

"His heart is yours, therefore it is yours to give."

Anise snarled and ran toward the throne, aiming for her dagger. The witch flicked her hand, and Anise went flying backward. She landed hard and skidded across the icy floor, groaning in pain. But if she couldn't get close to the witch, how could she defeat her?

Gaining the ability to shift wasn't worth Caraway's life. It wasn't worth his soul. She couldn't do this to him. Groaning, Anise clutched her side where the ice had bruised. She rolled and faced the ground then tried to crawl away from the witch, but only managed to get to the base of Caraway's icy tomb. She used the column to drag herself into a sitting position, then scowled at the witch.

"You tricked me," she accused. "You never said it had to be another's soul."

"I said *a* soul, dearie, not *your* soul. You clearly weren't listening hard enough. How do you think you'll gain the ability to shift? It has to come from somewhere."

"Still, why his? Why not someone else's?"

"Because he's the only one who belongs to you. He's the only one you have a right to give." The witch's brows rose. "Don't you see? My ability was stolen from me, but I took it back, plus more! You can finally be powerful. You can have them all whimpering at your feet. You can take what you want, just like they do."

Anise squeezed her eyes and shook her head. When she opened them, her gaze landed on Caraway's sword. Her mind blanked.

His sword.

Caraway had glanced at it before he'd frozen. Thinking back, it had been a purposeful glance. *A message?*

Take the weapon and use it.

But the sword was metal. Metal was forbidden because it halted the flow of mana through the earth, air, water, and through bodies of any fae. The sword would cut through any magic the witch threw Anise's way. It would cut through the witch. But just as the thoughts formed in her head, Anise felt disappointment crush her breath. Guardians were the only fae alive who could use metal weapons, and not disrupt their own flow of mana. Anyone else would experience extreme pain when using it.

But... she wasn't just anyone else.

She already had no mana. She couldn't shift. There was nothing in her body for the sword's metal to disrupt.

Caraway had known that. The look he'd given the sword *was* a message.

Hope flared. Anise licked her lips and glanced at the

witch. There was no way Anise could reach for the sword without the witch noticing. She would blast her with magic before Anise's fingers closed around the hilt. She had to trick her. She had to take a hit and fall within the range. The sword wasn't far, only a few feet to her right.

She steeled her resolve, hardened her gut, and growled before climbing to her feet, charging ahead but veering right. The witch threw out another hand of hard power. It knocked Anise senseless, and true to expectations, her body went flying backward again. The solid floor connected with Anise's shoulder. She cried out in pain, but went sliding backward, right within reach of the sword.

"When will you learn, little she-wolf?" the witch snarled.

Anise clutched her middle and feigned crawling away. Her body almost shielded her from view. As she reached for the giant sword, she had a moment of clarity. Caraway had been right. She didn't need the ability to shift. She was perfect the way she was. The very thing she'd cursed as lacking in her body was now the thing saving her life. It was all about perspective. No mana meant that when her fingers curled around the hilt of the magic-killing sword, she felt nothing but the overwhelming urge to protect what was hers.

She came to her feet, snarling and baring her teeth. Moving the sword to hold in two hands, she charged the dais using the sword as a shield. The witch tried to throw magic at Anise, but the sword cut it in half. The witch

tried to send ice through the ground, like she had Caraway, but he'd been taken by surprise. Anise didn't make the same mistake. She sliced and cut her way until she made it to the dais and launched up, taking the steps in two giant leaps. She aimed the tip of the sword straight forward and kept running as though carrying a lance. It pierced the witch through the heart, pinning her to her ice throne. Blood welled from the witch's mouth and she tried to scream. Only a gurgle came out.

"I'll learn when you're dead," Anise said and twisted the blade deep.

The witch's last gaze was at the fae she'd first encased in the ice, and it was a look of longing and regret. The pain froze in her expression as the light left her eyes, and Anise knew she'd made the right decision. If she'd accepted the bargain, Anise would have lived a life as lonely as the witch's. What were two hundred years if it was spent alone?

Sniffing, she wiped her nose on her sleeve, then yanked the sword out of the witch. The witch's body slumped down the throne and tumbled to the ground. Then Anise set to chipping away Caraway's tomb, praying to the Well that he would survive. It took long, drawn-out minutes, but she chipped enough for Caraway to break through. His big, powerful body exploded through the ice and he staggered to his knees with big, ragged breaths.

"Car," she said and fell to the ground with him.

He lifted his frost-covered chin and met her eyes. "You did it," he rasped. "I knew you would."

She sniffed and tried not to smile, but the pure adoration in his eyes warmed her heart.

She joked, "I guess having no mana counts for something right?"

The grin that split his blue lips was contagious. He cupped her jaw and brushed a trembling thumb along her skin. "Anise, you have something, or else you'd have aged at a human rate."

She blinked. "But I felt nothing when I touched the sword."

"The Well works in mysterious ways, and I can't explain it, but it's true. You have enough of the Well inside that you are fae. We can live here in Elphyne where the land flourishes. You don't have to manipulate the magic to appreciate it. As long as we're together, isn't that enough?"

She looked deep into his eyes. "Are we together?"

Worry flared in his gaze. "I hope so. I mean, I want to... don't you? That kiss... um."

His ears reddened and his cheeks reddened in a blush.

Well-damn, it was the most adorable thing she'd ever seen, and it gave her the courage to say, "I want to be more than together. I want to be mated with you."

CHAPTER 9

The sweetest words had come out of Anise's mouth, but Caraway couldn't give her the answer she needed. Not only was the cold in his system taking over, but he didn't know if mating was in his future as a Guardian.

He shivered uncontrollably. Concern replaced the light in Anise's eyes.

"We have to get you somewhere warm," she said.

He nodded. "P-Portal stone in my p-pocket-t."

She dug into his pants pocket and drew out a smooth stone that she placed in his cold, shaking fingers. He gave the frozen museum a scathing once-over—there had been no evidence that the witch had been working with the humans, but Caraway hadn't really had time to conduct a thorough investigation and those gargoyles definitely weren't natural.

Now he'd been here, he could create his own portal

stone back. All he needed was something native to the place.

"I need to c-collect some s-snow," he said. "F-for a portal stone."

Anise nodded and rifled around her bag for her waterskin. She emptied it and scooped some snow in. It would do.

He activated the portal, right there inside the hall. The transference of energy ripped a hole in space and time. He held out a hand to Anise. Before she took it, she collected her dagger from the throne and gave the dead witch one last look. Caraway thought he saw pity in her eyes and wondered what had transpired while he'd been frozen.

Then Anise took his hand and together they walked through the portal. They arrived not at the Order, as he'd thought, but on the snow-dusted sandy banks of a sacred lake near Rush's cabin. Rush and Clarke had lived here for two years while they raised their newborn away from society.

The sun dipped beyond the horizon, and darkness loomed.

Caraway searched in his pockets for the other portal stone, the one that would take them back to the Order, but Anise stopped him.

"Look," she said and pointed to the wooden cabin set near some trees.

Smoke curled from the chimney.

"It's Rush's c-cabin," he explained, still stuttering from

the cold. "Before I left the Order, Clarke s-sent me a portal stone that came here."

Anise grinned. "Gotta love that psychic human. Wish all of them were like her. It's getting dark and the cabin looks warm. Let's make camp for the night."

He gave her a quizzical look.

Anise elaborated. "Where there's smoke, there's fire. Come on. Let's get you warmed up."

She took his cold hand and pulled him toward the cabin. On the porch, they kicked the snow from their boots and then entered the one-room cabin. Inside was a bed, a kitchen counter, and a crackling fireplace with two small fire sprites dancing on a log to keep it smoldering. One male, one female. They paused upon Caraway's and Anise's entry and squeaked at the intrusion.

Caraway showed them the spent portal stone. "C-Clarke invited us."

The sprites—glowing red and orange figures made of flames—stared and then resumed their dancing, ignoring Anise and Caraway.

But the heat... it was divine.

Caraway shuffled closer to the fireplace and crouched low. He held his palms out and let the warmth suffuse his body, vaguely aware of Anise's bustling behind him in the kitchen. When she brought a ceramic pot filled with soup over to the fire, he realized she'd been cooking and a few minutes had gone by.

"There were root vegetables under the counter," she explained and placed the pot so it would cook.

The sprites grew curious and looked over the pot at the contents.

Once satisfied the sprites weren't going to cause mischief, Anise turned to Caraway with a determined look on her face.

"Time to get you out of the wet clothes."

His lips twitched. The fire was doing its job superbly at warming and drying him. He didn't need to, but he *wanted* to, so he let her systematically set about helping him out of his Guardian uniform. First, she removed his baldric and sword, then his boots. When she got to his jacket, he was already warmed up and getting hotter by the second. Her touch took the chill away more than any fire could.

This female, his friend who'd shared so much with him, was taking care of him. No one had done so since his youth—since before his mother and father had branded him as a violent anarchist.

This female, with whom he was irrevocably in love with, had saved his life.

He watched with reverence as she unpicked the bone-stud buttons down the center of his jacket.

Flickering firelight cast a glow on her face, softening her features. He found himself becoming breathless from her beauty. She felt her dark-rimmed eyes were too wolf-like, but he found them stunning. She hated the black smudge of color at the tip of her nose, but he wanted to lick it. She tried to hide her extra arched ears by wearing a leather cord around her head, but he smiled

where the ears stubbornly poked through the fall of black hair.

It was all Anise. It made her unique. It made her *more*, and it made her the one he loved.

She frowned as she peeled his jacket from his arms and shook it out. "It's so heavy and soggy," she murmured and then searched for a place to hang it. She found a hook on the back of the front door.

When she returned, she caught the heated look in Caraway's stare and blanched.

"What?" she asked. "Why are you staring?"

His lips curved on one side. "Because you're beautiful."

She ignored him and pointed at the rest of his wet clothes, his white shirt, and pants. "You should probably take it all off."

His grin widened and his laugh boomed out from deep in his belly. "You know, if you wanted to get my clothes off, there were easier ways of going about it than to get a witch to steal my soul."

It was meant to be a joke, but the pain in her eyes was real.

"Oh no," he murmured and reached for her hand. "I didn't mean it like that. It was a joke. Stupid."

Her lips flattened and she looked away. "I almost got you killed."

"I'm fine, Anise," he whispered. "And I'm not blameless here. I should have told you the truth about why I was with you. The Order may have given me the mission to follow you to the Ice-Witch, but it was because a prisoner

had mentioned her name during interrogation. I was too much of a coward to come and find you myself and, for that, I'll never be sorry enough. But let me be clear, I'm not sorry the mission brought me back to you."

After his words were done, silence hung in the air. Then she slowly lifted her gaze to his.

"You said 'sorry,'" she said.

He nodded. A spoken apology, or thank you, from one fae to another was an acknowledgment of debt. It gave a legally binding reason to forge a bargain to repay the debt. Caraway was essentially putting his life in Anise's hands. It was also known that debts were not acted on between family because they would do anything for their loved ones anyway.

How she responded would determine their future with each other.

"I'm sorry too," she said. "I should never have placed the blame on you for my capture two years ago, but you were the closest friend I had. You were the safest avenue. And if I didn't blame you, then I had to blame myself."

She flared her lashes in a way that made Caraway think she was trying not to cry, and when a tear spilled free anyway, it broke his heart.

He trailed a thumb across her cheek to wipe the moisture away. "Anise, what happened to you could have happened to anyone."

"But none of the shifters were caught." A sob wracked her body. "If I had the power, I could have protected myself."

"But you *can* protect yourself." He shook her gently. "You lived on your own in Cornucopia for years. You killed a troll and saved a baby. You bloody-well killed the Ice-Witch!" His eyes widened with the realization. "You're incredible, Anise. And you can't shift. You can't use mana to cast spells. So Well-damned what? You're *more* amazing for it."

He ran his hands down her arms and circled to her back where he let his touch glide down over the tail poking from her pants. She startled and looked up at him.

He grinned. "You can touch my horns."

It was meant to be a joke, to show that they were the same inside and out, but his voice came out low and rough, and once it emitted, he couldn't stop the train of his thoughts. Yes, he wanted her to touch him. Everywhere.

She licked his lips and then raked her heated gaze down his front. "That's not where I want to touch you."

His cock hardened instantly.

"Anise," he croaked, begged.

Her fingers curled beneath the hem of his shirt and lifted slowly. He sucked in a breath, abs curling inward, as her fingers brushed his stomach. She kept lifting. He raised his arms so she could remove his shirt, and then she started working on the drawstrings of his pants.

"Anise," he murmured.

"Shh," she scolded. "I'm enjoying this."

He was too, but desire raged inside him like an inferno. He was hard, tense, and coiled tight. When she

slid his pants down his thighs, her hair brushed his skin. He threw his head back and cursed loudly. Every time she touched him, his senses sparked like fireworks. She lifted each of his feet to slide his pants free, and when she was done, he scooped his hands under her arms and lifted her clear off the ground.

With a molten, golden gaze, she wrapped her legs around his waist and cupped his face to snarl against his lips. "Last chance, Car. Once I start this with you, I won't stop. I'll mark you as mine."

The wolf-shifters marked their mates to prove to the world they were together. The thought of her teeth on his neck ripped a growl of approval from his throat and he slammed his lips on hers, only pulling back to say, "I've always been yours. I'm ready."

CHAPTER 10

Anise sank her fangs into the thick column of Caraway's neck. Her hormones went haywire and a mating-musk scent seeped from her pores, coating Caraway. Usually, two shifters marked each other. Caraway wasn't a wolf, but he *was* fae, and mating in any fae race was classed as a serious union of commitment. He was ready. So was she.

She clutched him tightly as she bit down.

He moaned, his eyes rolled back, and he staggered toward the bed where he landed heavily with her on top of him. She laved at the wound she'd created with loving care and relished the evidence of their commitment. He didn't wait long before he started peeling her clothes from her body. First, her cape. Then her shirt, and then his thick fingers were digging into her pants, fumbling at the buttons.

Somehow, they managed to both end up completely

naked, sweaty, and in each other's arms. She thought she would be ashamed of being like this with him, but when he looked at her body... especially her breasts... his eyes heated with desire. A hungry growl rumbled from his throat and he latched onto her nipple, sucking greedily and sending showers of bliss coursing through her body.

They kissed and touched and played with each other, savoring this new level of intimacy. There was no doubt. He'd let her mark him, and from the way he fervently touched her and kissed her, it turned him on as much as it did her.

He rolled so he was on top and fit his hips between her legs. He took his erection in hand and entered her in one slick motion. She gasped, back bowing, as she adjusted to the sensation of him filling her. Moans and groans filled the room as they adjusted to the new onslaught of sensations, then he gave a self-satisfied masculine grunt and kissed her lips. Meeting her eyes, he braced his hands on either side of her head.

"You ready?" he asked, voice gravelly.

She lifted her hips. "Yes."

"I'm claiming you tonight, too. Are you ready?" he repeated, intense brown eyes pinned her so hard she lost her breath.

All she could do was nod and hold on as he pulled out and thrust back in until there was no doubt in her mind that he claimed her more thoroughly than any bite mark. Theirs was a claiming of hearts, bodies, and minds. Of futures and of pasts. Of wolves, fae, shifters, and ox. It

didn't matter what they looked like, only what they *felt*. Their love was forged from ice and fire, from kisses and wishes. And it was real.

ANISE WOKE ENTWINED with Caraway's muscular, naked body. She was so happy, she didn't want to leave, but one look at the black leather Guardian jacket hanging on the door hook reminded her of reality. They might have claimed each other, but it didn't mean the world would let them be together.

A Guardian warrior, and a lesser fae.

The world was full of cruel boundaries.

She sighed and rested her head on his shoulder. Her exhale ruffled the hair on his chest. His rumble of appreciation brought a smile to her lips so she ran her fingers through the coarse hair, wanting to elicit more sounds from her sleeping giant. His hand snapped up and swallowed hers whole, and then he directed it downward with a cheeky smirk, keeping his eyes closed the entire time.

"So demanding, already." She laughed.

He chuckled. It came from deep in his belly and sent Anise's hormones crazy. She'd always loved his laugh. It was so genuine, so real, and she never wanted to lose it again.

He must have sensed the change in her mood because when he looked down at her, a solemn shadow flittered in

his eyes. He rolled to face her and gently traced fingers down her arm.

"We'll figure it out, Anise," he promised.

"You can't quit being a Guardian." She touched the glowing blue teardrop tattoo beneath his right eye. "It's a part of you."

His brows joined in the middle. "So are you."

"How will we make this work, then?"

He shrugged. "Live with me at the Order."

"That's not possible."

"It is for Rush and Clarke, and Thorne and Laurel."

"But they're Well-blessed. Their union is honored above all else, especially by an organization that worships the Well."

"We don't worship it. We respect it and work to keeping it flourishing. There's a difference." Darkness formed in his eyes. "And I don't care if our union is blessed by the Well. I'm not leaving you again. They can all go and fu—"

"Shhh." She put a finger on his lips and sat up. Her ears twitched as she picked up voices. "Someone is outside."

She'd never seen Caraway move so fast, but within seconds, he was out of the bed. He threw a blanket over her and collected Reckoning. Heedless of his nudity, he went to the window and peered through. All the tension left his shoulders as his eyes latched onto their visitors, and then he turned back to her with confusion.

"It's Rush and Thorne."

She sat up with a squeak. "Don't let them inside until I'm dressed."

He went back to the window. "Clarke and Laurel are also here. And Willow."

"What?" Willow was Rush's and Clarke's small daughter.

Caraway nodded and slipped on his pants. "Maybe Clarke saw something in a vision. Could be why she sent me the portal stone. I'll go and greet them. You get dressed."

He put on his shirt and rested his sword by the door then went outside. While he was gone, Anise made quick work of clothing herself, and then straightened the cabin as much as she could. It wouldn't do to have the owner arrive and see it in such disarray. Thankfully the sprites had redirected the flames from burning the pot overnight. Only half of the wood smoldered. The soup was cold but not inedible. When she was done straightening the room, she put on her boots and ventured outside.

Fresh morning air greeted her. At least it wasn't snowing. Down on the shore of the lake, Caraway spoke with the two Guardians, while Laurel and Clarke collected stones with Willow by the waterside. Clarke's red hair was unmissable, and Laurel's dark bob just the same.

Anise didn't realize how tense she was until she saw the women were a distance away from her new mate. Her body viscerally relaxed, but the underlying protective mode was still there. It was a wolf instinct. She was sure it happened to the males of the species more, but she still had to make

an effort to calm herself down. When she had, a new kind of anxiety entered her system. She didn't know which group of visitors to go to first. She'd not truly met Laurel, but had served her at the Birdcage elixir den in Cornucopia.

Anise was saved from making her decision when Willow spotted she was out of the cabin, squealed, and ran toward her with unrestrained delight. Anise had not formally met the little girl either but had heard about her stark white hair from Thorne. She was a halfling—half wolf-shifter, half-human—but one-hundred percent tenacious.

Willow's little legs brought her closer to Anise with every squeal. As she neared, Anise recognized the squeals were words.

"Gray is coming. Gray is coming!" Willow barreled past Anise and up to the cabin porch where she grinned and whirled around, hiding behind a wooden pole, intently watching the horizon of the nearby woods where an old wolf emerged, sniffed the air, and then spotted Rush. He trotted over, sniffed him too, and then yipped before heading up to the cabin to meet Willow.

"He's getting old," Clarke noted as she arrived and gave the wolf a pointed look. "He was Rush's long time companion when he was cursed, and he protected our cabin while Willow was a baby. This might be the last time she will get to see her old protector."

"Oh, that's sad," Anise replied.

Clarke gave Anise a gentle smile. "It is, but it's the

natural order of life for those animals, and humans for that matter. Any creature without mana in them ages so fast. I'm still getting used to the idea that I'm not one of them anymore. Anyway, it's good to see you, Anise."

Caraway had said something similar to Anise back at the witch's lair. If Anise was truly without mana, she'd have aged a long time ago. Somehow, knowing that made Anise feel warm inside. She smiled at Clarke. "It's good to see you too."

Clarke gestured to Laurel. "I think you might have met Laurel."

"Sort of."

Laurel bit her lip. "Yeah, that's my fault. I was a bit preoccupied the last time we met." She made the fae hand-sign for an apology—a fist in circles over her chest. "It was rude of me."

Anise laughed it off. "You weren't rude. I was the barmaid. I served you a drink. That's all."

"Yes, well, if it's all the same to you, if I hadn't been so angry at Thorne, I would have taken the time to give you a proper hello."

Clarke waggled her brows at Anise. "I see my little gift went to good use?"

"Gift?" Anise frowned.

Clarke tapped a bite mark scar on her own neck. Laurel laughed and tapped her own. Then they both made eyes at Caraway's fresh mating mark.

"Oh!" Anise blushed. "You saw us getting together in a

vision? Is that why you gave him the portal stone for here? How embarrassing."

"Not at all!" Clarke replied. "Actually, we're here for another reason."

Anise cocked a brow.

"What reason?" Caraway asked as the Guardians arrived.

Laurel took Thorne's hand, and Anise couldn't help noticing the matching blue markings entwining both their arms. Rush and Clarke had similar identical markings on their hands. They were magnificent. Like water reflections living on their skin.

"I wanted to thank you for helping me out when I first arrived. Waking up two thousand years after my time wasn't so easy to deal with. And this lout didn't make it easier at the start," Clarke said, pointing to Rush who grunted irritably. She laughed. "Anise, you and Caraway were so kind to me that night in the tavern. So—" She shared a conspiring look with Laurel. "We've come up with a solution that keeps you two together."

Thorne frowned. "I told them they were meddling."

Rush also clenched his jaw. "But it's a good idea."

"What?" Anise asked. "Don't keep us in suspense."

Laurel grinned. "I've been working with the Prime to raise the public profile of the Order. Too many fae-folk don't look favorably on the organization and it's been a real problem lately. High King Mithras is gaining power, and it's not good. So I've convinced the Prime to station trusted Guardians in cities and towns around Elphyne so

the Order always has a point of contact for anyone with questions. No more mystery. I think if we make each Guardian seem more approachable, like an ambassador as well as a protector, then more fae will want to volunteer to be initiated. The Order won't need to seek tributes from children anymore."

Thorne squeezed her shoulder and a look of sheer pride crossed his face.

"What does that mean for us?" Caraway asked.

"It means," Rush elaborated. "The two of you can live together in a city of your choice. Caraway won't need to live at the Order grounds, and instead of heading out into the wild on missions, he can work at improving the Order's image in the city he's stationed at."

"Couldn't think of a better Guardian for the job." Thorne clapped Caraway on the back.

"We can be together?" Anise could hardly believe it. Caraway could stay a Guardian, and they could stay together.

Their eyes met, held, and then Caraway rushed to pick her up in a bone-crushing hug. Her mind whirled. Could it be that simple?

He put her down, eyes searching hers. "Where do you want to live?"

Immediately, her heart took her home, to Crescent Hollow. But the familiar pang and panic of her attack left her mouth dry at the thought of returning there.

No, she told herself. This time it was different. *She* was different. She had to stop letting her fears take hold of

her. Sure, she'd had bad memories there, but there had also been good memories. And fae lived a long time... possibly forever. Hopefully, she and Caraway would share a long life together. She smiled up at him and for the first time in a long time, wanted to go home.

"Let's go to Crescent Hollow."

He grinned back at her. "I was hoping you would say that."

Rush cleared his throat. "Let's go inside and you can tell us about the Ice-Witch while Willow plays with Gray. Thorne and I will take your intel and the sample of snow back to the Prime. Your mission is done, Caraway."

Clarke stopped her mate with a hand to the shoulder. "Let's just get the snow sample. I think the newly mated couple might want to spend some alone time together."

Rush's eyes widened when he caught the fresh mark on Caraway's neck. A blush hit his cheeks. Both he and Thorne quickly made excuses to leave. Both were so rushed, she knew they were contrived, but was grateful all the same.

Anise smiled when she looked at her new friends and realized just how far she'd come. No longer did those taunts from her memories haunt her because Anise *did* have friends. She had a lover. A mate. And she had a future. It didn't matter what she looked like on the outside. It only mattered how she lived her life and the love she invited in. That jaded Ice-Witch had it all wrong.

Anise looked up into Caraway's eyes, she knew her life

would be the opposite of lonely. It would be filled with love, kisses, and wishes come true.

The End.

Catch up with more Fae Guardians on Amazon Kindle, or visit Lana's website for more details on other editions.

FIRST TIME IN ELPHYNE?

Check out the Fae Guardians from book one in Kindle Unlimited. You'll get plenty of growling protective fae mates, women who find their power within, angst, tension, and always spicy romance.

Season of the Wolf Trilogy
1. The Longing of Lone Wolves
2. The Solace of Sharp Claws
2.5 Of Kisses & Wishes Novella (standalone novella)
3. The Dreams of Broken Kings

Season of the Vampire Trilogy
4. The Secrets in Shadow and Blood
5. A Labyrinth of Fangs and Thorns
6. A Symphony of Savage Hearts

Season of the Elf Trilogy
    7. A Song of Sky and Sacrifice
    7.5 Of Pixies and Promises (standalone novella)
    8. A Crown of Cruel Lies
    9. A War of Ruin and Reckoning

JOIN LANA'S VIPS

On Facebook? Join Lana's Angels Reader Group https://www.facebook.com/groups/lanasangels

ALSO BY LANA PECHERCZYK

FAE GUARDIANS WORLD

Fae Guardians Series

(For Witcher and ACOTAR fans who want more spice)

Season of the Wolf Trilogy

The Longing of Lone Wolves

The Solace of Sharp Claws

Of Kisses & Wishes Novella (free for subscribers)

The Dreams of Broken Kings

Season of the Vampire Trilogy

The Secrets in Shadow and Blood

A Labyrinth of Fangs and Thorns

A Symphony of Savage Hearts

Season of the Elf Trilogy

A Song of Sky and Sacrifice

A Crown of Cruel Lies

A War of Ruin and Reckoning

THE DEADLYVERSE

The Deadly Seven

(For Marvel fans who want more spice)

The Deadly Seven Box Set Books 1-3

Sinner (prequel origins novella)

Envy

Greed

Wrath

Sloth

Gluttony

Lust

Pride

Despair

The Sinner Sisterhood

(For fans of Supernatural and Buffy)

The Sinner and the Scholar

The Sinner and the Gunslinger

ABOUT THE AUTHOR

OMG! How do you say my name?

Lana (straight forward enough - Lah-nah) **Pecherczyk** (this is where it gets tricky - Pe-her-chick).

I've been called Lana Price-Check, Lana Pera-Chickywack, Lana Pressed-Chicken, Lana Pech...*that girl!* You name it, they said it. So if it's so hard to spell, why on earth would I use this name instead of an easy pen name?

To put it simply, it belonged to my mother. And she was my dream champion.

For most of my life, I've been good at one thing – art. The world around me saw my work, and said I should do more of it, so I did.

But, when at the age of eight, I said I wanted to write stories, and even though we were poor, my mother came home with a blank notebook and a pencil saying I should follow my dreams, no matter where they take me for they will make me happy. I wasn't very good at it, but it didn't matter because I had her support and I liked it.

She died when I was thirteen, and left her four daughters orphaned. Suddenly, I had lost my dream champion, I was split from my youngest two sisters and had no one to talk to about the challenge of life.

So, I wrote in secret. I poured my heart out daily to a diary and sometimes imagined that she would listen. At the end of the day, even if she couldn't hear, writing kept that dream alive.

Eventually, after having my own children (two firecrackers in the guise of little boys) and ignoring my inner voice for too long, I decided to lead by example. How could I teach my children to follow their dreams if I wasn't? I became my own dream champion and the rest is history, here I am.

When I'm not writing the next great action-packed romantic novel, or wrangling the rug rats, or rescuing GI Joe from the jaws of my Kelpie, I fight evil by moonlight, win love by daylight and never run from a real fight.

I live in Australia, but I'm up for a chat anytime online. Come and find me.

Subscribe & Follow

subscribe.lanapecherczyk.com

lp@lanapecherczyk.com

- facebook.com/lanapecherczykauthor
- instagram.com/lana_p_author
- amazon.com/-/e/B00V2TP0HG
- bookbub.com/profile/lana-pecherczyk
- tiktok.com/@lanapauthor
- goodreads.com/lana_p_author

KISSES
AND
WISHES